AMBUSH CREEK

Center Point
Large Print

**This Large Print Book carries the
Seal of Approval of N.A.V.H.**

AMBUSH CREEK

Phil Dunlap

CENTER POINT LARGE PRINT
THORNDIKE, MAINE

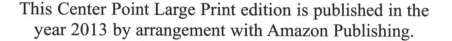

Library of Congress Cataloging-in-Publication Data

Dunlap, Phil.
Ambush Creek / Phil Dunlap.
pages ; cm.
ISBN 978-1-61173-708-0 (library binding : alk. paper)
1. Missing persons—Fiction. 2. Bounty hunters—Fiction.
    3. Large type books. I. Title.
PS3604.U548A84 2013
813′.6—dc23
                                        2012050103

To my loving wife, family, and friends
who continue to encourage me.
Without every one of you,
I would count it all for naught.

Chapter One

Cochise, Arizona Territory 1880

Sheriff John Henry Stevens leaned on the door frame of his office looking out on the main street of Cochise, Arizona Territory. He was sipping the remains of the coffee he'd made earlier in the morning and hating every drop. It was strong, bitter, and cold. But the sheriff lived strictly by the code he'd been taught by his father: Waste not, want not. Sheriff Stevens wasted nothing. Ever. It was a deeply ingrained principle he could not abandon, and everybody knew it. He wore his britches until the seat was shiny and nearly threadbare. His socks had been darned so many times, they were more string than weave. When he made a pot of coffee, he'd consume every last drop until he came up with a mouthful of dregs. Some folks snickered behind his back, but none made it an issue. After all, his salary, as small as it was, came to him by way of the town council, and those esteemed gentlemen, ever conscious of the pitfalls of financial mismanagement, were always vocally appreciative of his conservative ways.

Today, however, the sheriff wasn't thinking about ways to save the town money. Rather, his thoughts were on the three scruffy men who'd ridden into Cochise a half hour earlier. He'd stood watching as they dismounted, looked around suspiciously, and then tied their horses to the rail in front of the saloon. They'd stomped inside, without even the basic courtesy of dusting themselves off first. In the sun's glare and at a distance of a half block away, not one of the men was familiar to him. He was struck with a disagreeable degree of foreboding from little more than the brief glimpse of them—rough, dirty, unshaven, and carrying enough lethal hardware for a small army. A chill ran up his back as he considered the potential for disaster that could be leveled on his quiet town if they should decide to unleash their firepower.

After the three disappeared inside the saloon, he'd returned to his desk to begin shuffling through the stack of WANTED dodgers he'd stuffed in a drawer. None of the men appeared to be wanted—a fact he found difficult to believe, considering the look of them. He knew he should stroll over to the saloon to size up that bunch, since he really hadn't gotten a good look. He was certain they must be on the run from something. His better judgment was the only thing keeping him in his office.

They haven't caused any trouble yet. No

reason for me to go stickin' my nose into another man's business if it don't concern me, he thought. Besides, truth be known, he was pretty certain, given his age and all, he'd likely end up on the wrong end of a bullet if the three of them took offense at his presence. He returned to his chair, leaned back, and shut his eyes. *A little snooze won't hurt none, and it might just settle my nerves.*

He'd no more than closed his eyelids than it started. It was nothing more than a single gun-shot; then all manner of whooping and hollering erupted, and it was coming from the saloon. Stevens' worst fears had been realized. The three scruffy owl-hoots were making themselves known in a most uncivilized way. Stevens got up, buckled on his six-shooter, and grabbed a coach gun from the rack. He broke the breach, loaded two double-ought buckshot shells into it, and snapped it closed. He remembered to take his hat from the peg near the door to protect his head from the blazing sun, although he wasn't sure it would make any real difference for the fifty-foot trip to the saloon. But his balding head had been exposed too often to the scorching rays of old Sol, searing his skin with blisters, and he wasn't about to go anywhere uncovered anytime soon.

When the sheriff reached the swinging doors to the saloon, he looked over the top to get an idea of what he might find himself confronted with.

What he saw surprised him. All three of the rough- looking men were sitting around a table, engulfed in a cloud of hazy smoke, drinks in front of them, and one man seemed to be taking bets on his ability to hit something on the floor near the rear of the room. Several patrons were standing around, cheering the man on. He already had a pile of money in front of him and was about to take a shot, aiming carefully by bracing one hand with the other. The smoke that hovered above the table made seeing each man clearly next to impossible.

"Now, hold on, gents, we can't have no shootin' in town. Don't you know that?" Stevens said, his words bringing a sudden silence to the room as he strolled closer.

The man with the gun looked up briefly, then said, "Don't you worry none, Sheriff, one more shot will do it for sure. I never miss." And he squeezed off a blast that rattled the windows. A roar went up from the few other patrons.

Sheriff Stevens stomped over to the table. "Didn't you hear what I said, mister?"

"Yep, I heard you, Sheriff, but I had a bet to complete. You walk over there to the wall and verify that I hit what I was aimin' at. Then I can collect my money, and all the hoopla will be done with. They'll take a lawman's word for it."

Stevens frowned at the man. But his curiosity was about to overwhelm him, so he decided to humor the man a bit longer. As he neared the back wall, he bent down to see two holes in the floor right at the bottom of the wall. One was nothing more than a hole, where a bullet had plowed into the soft pine, splintering the baseboard, plain and simple. The other included what was left of a mouse, its body all but decimated by the large-caliber bullet.

He looked over at the man and said, "I don't know what's goin' on here, but there are better ways to rid the joint of vermin. Does one of you want to explain?"

"Why, sure, Sheriff. We're just a bunch of fun-lovin' cowpokes with a sense of humor. That's all there is to tell. And, of course, like most cowpokes, we do like to engage in a small wager now and again." The man reached over and scraped all the money that lay on the table into his hat. With a huge, yellow-toothed grin, he thanked his shooting opponent. What he got back was a look of defiance and eyes that narrowed to suggest he hadn't seen the last of it. "Ike, here, got the first shot and missed. Then it was my turn."

"And that little show of gunmanship was what won you all that money?"

"Yep. Sheriff, I assume there's no law in town about shootin' them furry pests, is there?"

"No, I reckon not, as long as it stops there. We're a peaceable little community, and the sound of gunfire just naturally gets folks upset. So, if you fellas wouldn't mind, how about I take your guns over to my office, and you can pick 'em up when you're ready to leave? No hurry, though. Stay as long as you like. But I'd be obliged if you'd just hand over your gun belts, and we'll call it a day. While we're at it, if you see another mouse, I'd be gratified if you'd settle for throwin' rocks at it." Stevens stood his ground, bringing the shotgun to bear just enough to make his point, while the three men looked first at one another and then to the one who appeared to be their leader. They were obviously looking for some sign as to whether to comply with the sheriff's order or not. The issue was settled when the bartender also placed a shotgun on the bar and cocked it.

"All right boys, let's go along with the sheriff this time. We ain't goin' to be here that long anyhow, and I don't figure we're goin' to be needin' our shootin' irons before we ride out." The men grumbled a bit as they unbuckled their guns and handed them over.

With a tip of his hat, Sheriff Stevens left the saloon and, perspiring profusely from the tension of facing three gunmen alone, went straight to his office to brew some more of his double-strength coffee to settle his nerves. He piled the three gun belts on a table, then slid into his chair with a sigh.

"Land a'mighty, I'm gettin' way too old for this nonsense," he mumbled.

"Now, what'd you let that old fool sheriff take our guns for, Snake?" asked one of the men Stevens had confronted moments earlier at the saloon. The man called Snake slapped the other man across the face with his hat so fast, the others were startled, each instinctively making a grab for their guns, which, thanks to the sheriff, were no longer on their hips.

"Stop callin' me Snake, you damned fool," the man hissed just loudly enough to be heard by the other two and no one else. "Someone's gonna figure out who we are, and they may not take kindly to bounty hunters."

"But we *are* bounty hunters, and it's hard to forget that. It's sorta stuck in my head, that's all. Won't happen again, Sna—er, sorry." The man hung his head from the embarrassment of being struck and his stumbling attempt to remember what he was being chastised for in the first place.

"It better not. If anyone finds out bounty hunters are in the Territory, we'll be runnin' all the way to the big ocean before we can let up. Lots of folks don't take kindly to three men haulin' off their kinfolk, 'specially them with a questionable past. You boys *do* see the problem here, don't you?" Snake said in just above a whisper.

The others nodded their understanding as the one called Snake got up and sauntered to the bar. His face was homely, long, and gaunt, with close-set eyes and large ears. His deep voice, however, carried with it an expectation that he be heard.

"I 'spect you know just about everybody around here for fifty miles, am I right?" Snake asked the bartender.

"I reckon I know most, yep. Why do you ask?"

"Well, we're wantin' to look up an old friend. His name is Bowdre, Alex Bowdre. We're told he lives near here."

The bartender stopped wiping a glass, set it on the bar, then rubbed his chin for a moment as his gaze wandered across the ceiling. "Well, I ain't certain, you understand, but I seem to recollect a fella named Alex ownin' a ranch just up the road. But his name is Alex Bond, so I doubt that's the same fella."

"Where can we find this Bond?"

"Got a spread up near Apache Wells, 'bout ten, fifteen miles due north. That's about all I can tell you. But, as I say, I doubt he'd be the fella you're lookin' for."

"We'll look in on him just the same. Thanks, friend."

Snake motioned for the others to follow him outside.

"We'll go down to the livery and see if we can

stay in the loft for the night. Reckon it's time we paid more attention to savin' money where we can before we up and find ourselves flat busted," Snake said. He started down the street with the other two following, each mumbling to himself in obvious disagreement over the suggested sleeping arrangements. No one openly made an issue of it, however, and Snake led his procession of gunslingers down the center of the street.

A somewhat nervous Sheriff Stevens watched from a distance.

Chapter Two

The three men managed to convince the livery-man to allow them a free night's stay in the loft at the town's one and only livery and corral. Two of the men had voted to stay the night in the saloon, mostly drinking and sleeping with their heads on the table, but Snake wouldn't hear of it. As he'd said, they had too little money, and that meant for whiskey too. Since they were all cold sober at dawn's first light, they brushed the straw off their clothes and came calling on Sheriff Stevens to collect their guns. He jumped at the sound of their boots stomping through the door. They pushed it open so hard, the glass rattled. He'd fallen asleep in his chair with his feet up on his desk, a position he'd remained in all night, instead of his usual use of a slightly more comfortable bunk in one of his two cells.

"Wh-What the devil! What do you fellas think you're doin' here this early in the mornin'?" Stevens said, blinking and wiping the sleep from his eyes and attempting to stretch out the kinks in his back from his poor choice of sleeping arrangements. The bright sun coming through the window put the men in near silhouette, making them all but indistinguishable.

"We just come to collect our shootin' irons, Sheriff. We'll be a-movin' on. That's all."

"Hmm. Well, all right. Your guns are right over there on that table. You realize that by pickin' up your arms, you gotta be leavin' town right now. No lingerin' or pussyfootin' around."

"We understand, Sheriff, and we thank you for keepin' our six-shooters safe from any desperate locals who might take it into their minds to pilfer 'em. And since we don't figure to come this way again, we'll be sayin' adios." The three picked up their guns and holsters, strapped them on, and left without another word. Stevens sat with his mouth open, scratching his head as he heard them mount up and ride out.

He went to the window to make sure they followed through as they'd said they would. When they cleared the town and turned north, Stevens poured himself some cold coffee and stepped outside to sit beneath the overhang. He sat, leaning against the clapboard siding, and sipped for several minutes before his curiosity finally got the best of him. *What were they here for in the first place? They didn't 'pear to be looking for jobs. In fact, they looked more like troublemakers.* That possible revelation didn't set right with the grizzled old sheriff. He put his cup down beside his chair, got up, and ambled to the saloon. *Maybe I'll find some answers there,* he thought. As he was wool-gathering, completely oblivious to the world around him, he was almost run down by a fast-moving livery wagon that slid around the corner just as he passed the middle of the street.

"Why don't you watch where you're goin, you darn fool? Someone could get hurt, the way you're drivin' that thing!" shouted Stevens. He shook a fist at the young man wielding the reins of the two-horse team. He continued on, none the worse for wear, other than being a little dustier than when he started out, but in a decidedly nastier mood. He entered the saloon to find it as empty as Lazarus' tomb. When he called out to Joe, he was greeted by the unshaven bartender as he emerged from the back room where he slept, pulling up his suspenders and scratching his head.

"Where is everybody, Joe? They all get spooked by the remains of that rodent in the corner? When you gonna clean that thing up?"

"I figured if I leave it there long enough, it might serve as a warning to the rest of them var-mints that it ain't safe to hang around saloons." The bartender chuckled. He had also gone to bed last night without restocking two crates of bottles that remained stacked behind the bar.

"What d'ya figure them boys was doin' in Cochise?"

"Said they were lookin' for some fella named Alex Bowdre."

"Hmm. There ain't no Bowdre around here as I recollect. What'd you tell 'em?"

"Told 'em just that—don't know of any Bowdres at all. I did say there was a fella named Alex Bond up north of here, though. But I doubted that was the same man they was lookin' for," Joe said.

"Wonder what they wanted that Bowdre for."

"Can't say. I can only venture a guess."

"What's that?" Stevens asked.

"If I was to get to thinkin' on it real hard, I'd figure them three were bounty hunters, that's what."

"Did you hear any names?"

"I think one of 'em called another one Snake. Didn't mean anything to me."

That got the sheriff's attention. He slammed a fist on the bar so hard, Joe nearly dropped a bottle. "That's it! That must have been the mouthy one, the one that took his shot even after I warned him against it. I'll bet anything that was Snake Torres. He *is* a bounty hunter, and one lowdown, back-shootin' polecat. I never met up with him before, but I've heard of him."

"Sounds like you was lucky you didn't have to tangle with him, 'specially since he had two other rattlers to back his play."

"You're darn right about that, Joe," Stevens said, brushing away a stream of perspiration that had started down his forehead at the recognition of Torres' name.

"Maybe it's time you look to replace that deputy you had that went bad. You could use some backup, old friend," Joe said. His expression not only showed concern for the sheriff's well-being but also questioned his judgment in not getting help after his previous deputy turned out to be a thief and a murderer. Any town in the Arizona Territory that had only one lawman, and an aging one at that, was just plain asking for trouble from the dozens of rabble-rousers and misfits that rode in almost every day.

"I 'spect you got a point there, Joe. I'll think on it," Stevens said with a sigh. He turned and struck out for the jail to brew up another pot of coffee to help keep him awake the rest of the day. *The way I'm feelin' right now, I'd best be thinkin' on it right seriously too.*

When he got back to his chair—a captain's chair with leather padding and an extra pillow to help cushion his bony rear end—he started shuffling through his records to see if there might be any mention of Snake Torres and any problems that might be attached to the name. He thumbed through page after page with nothing that referenced the man. He stacked his hands on the pile of paper and stared at the dirty window, his tired eyes surrounded by a tired face.

"What do we do if this Bond fella ain't the one we're after, Snake?" asked one of the three bounty hunters.

"After ridin' all the way from Santa Fe in

search of Bowdre, I reckon I'm of a mind not to be all that particular whether he is or he ain't, Ike. If he's close, I might be tempted to take him anyway." Snake grinned big, revealing what few teeth he still had in his head, all of them yellowed from tobacco and strong coffee.

"That don't seem too smart. We don't even have any idea what this Bowdre looks like. If we start draggin' the wrong man into some sheriff's office and demandin' to get paid for it, there's sure to be a howl from the man that's been wronged, don't you figure?"

"A man with a bullet in his skull don't do a whole lot of howlin', Ike."

"You sayin' we just plug 'im and take him in across his saddle? Don't we ask questions first? What if we happen on a man what ain't never done a wrong thing in his life?"

"Now, have you ever run across a man who ain't broke at least one law? Huh?"

Ike slumped in the saddle, his mouth all screwed up, thinking as hard as he was capable of thinking, trying to come up with someone, anyone, that he knew was clean as a whistle when it came to being a true law-abiding citizen. He puzzled on that for several minutes while Snake and the other one rolled their eyes at each other and snickered.

Ike mumbled something about it sounding like nothing short of murder to him and that could get a man a rope necktie, but the others ignored him and spurred their mounts on down the road. They'd gone approximately fifteen miles, give or take, according to Snake's calculations, which were based solely on how sore his bottom was getting, when they drew up under some mesquite trees.

"That looks like a ranch house over there, beyond that stand of willows. We'll see if that's the place we're lookin' for. If not, they'll surely know how much farther it is to the Bond spread."

They followed a winding trail that led to a clapboard house, a barn, and a small corral. The house sat on a little rise with a creek wandering through the side yard. They pulled up in front of the house, and Snake cupped a hand to his mouth and called out.

"Hello, the house. Anyone home?"

His shout was greeted by a rifle shot that struck the ground not ten feet in front of his horse. The horse shied, nearly tossing the startled rider off. Snake held up a hand.

"Hold on, friend, we ain't here lookin' for no trouble. We'd just like a word with whoever owns the place. We're peaceable." He raised his hands to indicate that he wasn't going for his gun, as he looked quickly around at the two others to make sure they hadn't armed themselves in response to the rancher's gunshot.

In a minute a rangy man stepped out onto the porch, still holding his rifle, which was pointed squarely at the three. "Speak your piece, and then be off with you!" the man shouted. "I got no time for palaverin' with a bunch of saddle tramps."

That remark set Snake's teeth on edge. He didn't care for folks disparaging his looks or demeanor. Trying to keep calm so as not to spook the man, he kept his hands crossed on the saddle horn, cleared his throat, and spoke with no malice in his voice.

"Sorry to bother you, stranger, but we are looking for the Bond place and thought to stop here for directions. We don't know the country hereabouts."

"What is it you want with Bond?"

"Why, er, we were hopin' he might know a fella named Bowdre, Alex Bowdre, late of New Mexico. He has a brother over there name of Charlie Bowdre, although I must sadly announce ol' Charlie has met with a sad end," Snake said, glancing quickly at the ground as if he were trying to be reverent, which was near to an impossibility for a man with his low morals.

"Never heard of anyone named Bowdre. Now, git!" The man slammed the door, startling the riders' horses.

"Damn! Now, that was sure unfriendly, wouldn't you fellas say? What say we throw a few shots his way just to let him know we got our feelin's hurt?" Snake said as he drew his revolver, took aim, and began showering the door with lead. His companions followed suit.

When their guns were empty, Snake called out, "Hey, you inside, don't make us come in and drag you out here. I aim to take this Bowdre back to New Mexico for robbery. Got a hefty price on his head. I figure you know a mite more'n you let on. Make it easy on yourself."

The only response from the house was a shot from a Winchester rifle that came so close to Snake's head, he could feel the breeze as it went by. He dove from his saddle, landing on the ground in a cloud of dirt. His companions whirled their horses around and lit a shuck for the cover of boulders some twenty yards away, while Snake struggled to get to his feet and remount his skittish horse. The horse took off to rejoin the others, with Snake racing after it, dodging and weaving in case the man inside the house had taken a bead on him again. When he reached the relative safety of the boulders where the others were hunkered down, he was puffing and panting from getting more exercise than he could remember since he was a teenager.

"Looks like that fella don't want to be taken in for no reward, Snake. Best we think about goin' back to town to reconsider the plan. Looks like robbin' the bank might be easier."

Ike's comment was greeted by an angry sneer from Snake. He drew his rifle from its scabbard. "Load up, boys. I don't aim for this hombre to get out of here alive."

Chapter Three

Gilded Lily Mine, Desert Belle, Arizona Territory

"Miz McQueen, I've gone over the books for the past year, and I feel certain this is our best course of action. It's the only way for us to get out of debt. I figure the new partner would want you to stay on as manager, although I can't vouch for that, since I never met the man," Abner Dillard said.

"What *do* we know about this fellow?"

"We know he's offered to pay $50,000 for a fifty-five percent share of the Gilded Lily. He says if you'll send him a letter of intent to sell a partnership in the mine and its assets, he will, at the time of the transaction, deposit the money in the Desert Belle First Drover's Bank. Says he guarantees it."

"And you've never met him?"

"No, ma'am. Just know him from his inquiries as to the solvency of the Lily and follow-ups after I answered his inquiry."

"What did you tell him?"

"Well, I figured the truth can never hurt you. We are in dire need of working capital. His offer is a fair one, considerin' the shape we're in. Fiscally speakin', of course. If we don't do somethin', we'll be out of business in two months."

Molly McQueen sat down in a leather-covered camp chair that sat next to Dillard's tall bookkeeper's desk. Dillard stood with a pen in hand. The company ledger was spread open on the desktop. Molly looked at the ledger forlornly. She shook her head, her graying hair a tangle of loose curls. Molly wasn't much for dressing up. Her life had been a hard one, starting with the death of her husband several years back at the hands of an Indian raiding party. She'd turned to being a mule skinner because that's what her husband had been, driving freight wagons, and that was about all she knew. She had no time for frilly, feminine things, not that she didn't appreciate a touch of perfume or a piece of lace now and again. When the former owner of the Lily had been shot down by U.S. Marshal Piedmont Kelly for the wanton murder of a deputy sheriff, the bank, which held the deed to the Lily, had decided to give her a chance to make the business work. She'd paid back the bank all that the Lily owed within six months and had seemed to be headed for a banner year. But now Abner Dillard was saying she was nearly broke.

Having never been trained in bookkeeping, Molly was forced to rely on the good judgment of those who had been. Abner Dillard had come highly recommended by the bank management and the town's only attorney, J. Franklin Bottomwell. She stared at the worn floor and the tiny spots of ink that had splashed there when-ever Abner cleaned his pens. She sighed heavily.

"I reckon you know what you're talking about, Abner. I don't doubt those columns of numbers and such, but I'll never understand how it could come on us so sudden like. Seems to me our shipments have been increasing, not the other way around."

"Yes, ma'am, I surely do understand. To one untrained in the fine art of keeping an accurate and comprehensive accounting, it's likely to appear that way. But, in actuality, business has been off over forty percent. The mine has been slipping slowly for several months now, and the chances of it ever recovering on its own, without an infusion of money, is doubtful. It is my humble opinion that you should accept Mr. Bond's offer."

"Have you looked into this fella's honesty, his ability to come up with the promised amount?"

"Yes, ma'am. I've looked into every nook and cranny, trying to sniff out any irregularities. I can find nothing to suggest he won't come through as he has promised. He says if we send him the letter, he's promised to have the money deposited into the bank the very next day by return stage-coach."

"How can he do that? Is he in Desert Belle?"

"Uh, well, I figure he'll be comin' to town to wrap up the deal."

"Then I'd like to meet him before we sign any papers." Molly crossed her arms and set her jaw. A determined look pushed her lips tightly together.

"I can ask, but he said he was interested only if you are willing to take him on his word that he'll deliver."

"Just why should I send this letter to him without a guarantee of his compliance?" Molly's expression of dismay turned to one of apprehension.

"I been thinkin' some on that very thing. And I believe I have a way for it to all be taken care of, right and proper, so you won't have any worries. I'll ride into Desert Belle as soon as you send the letter off. I'll wait for the stage to deliver the money from Mr. Bond's bank. We'll put a binder in the letter that says the deal is null and void if the money doesn't arrive within three days. And there'll be no deal without us havin' the money in hand. I'll be there to see it happens just that way. How's that sound to you, ma'am?"

"I reckon that'd be all right. I'll send the letter of intent to the Tucson post office, box ten, like you told me. I'll let you know as soon as it's on the stage. You can plan to go into town to wait for the money tomorrow or the next day." Molly got up slowly and shuffled to the door. She let herself out, letting the door bang shut behind her. She was nearly in tears. It seemed as if all her hard work and efforts to keep a tight rein on the operation had been for naught. It was a damned shame, that's what it was.

She went to her office and locked the door. She needed some time to herself to think this whole thing out. *I could have sworn we were doing great things here at the Lily. Now I question why the bank put its faith in me, of all people. Why didn't they just run it themselves? Why trust all this to an old mule skinner? A nobody without the brains to know failure from success?*

She opened the safe and took out the deed to the Gilded Lily. Right beside it was the .41-caliber derringer she kept there for protection, although it had been sitting there, untouched, ever since she came to the Lily over a year ago. She picked it up, giving brief thought to using it on herself. After all, it was obvious she was of no use to the mine, or to her employees, or even to herself anymore. *Why not?* she thought. *Who'll give a hoot one way or another?*

But as quickly as the thought presented itself, it vanished with a sharp self-recrimination. *What am I thinking? Only an old fool would consider suicide as a logical alternative to facing your problems head-on. Nope, I'll ride this one out just as I rode out all those years after my poor husband was murdered by savages*. She pushed the little gun back into the safe and closed the door, locking it with a twist of the combination wheel.

She sat at her own desk and opened the deed. She read it over a couple of times. It was a bearer deed. That meant that the legal owner of the mine was whoever was in possession of the deed. That was the way the deed was originally written when the mine was owned by King Slaughter, purchased with the bank's money. When Slaughter was killed, the bank owned the mine by virtue of possession of the deed, since Slaughter hadn't paid off his note, and he had no relatives. When she took control of it after she had been able to pay off the bank's note, it became hers, for all intents, since she had the deed in her physical possession. Now it was about to be shared with someone else, and all because she hadn't paid close enough attention to the financial end of her responsibilities. At least that's what she believed. She'd been raised to be responsible for her own actions, and since she had been in charge at the time the mine began to lose money, then by rights she was at fault for any failures that might ensue.

She sat staring out the one window her office had. It looked out over the road back to Desert Belle. The scene brought back memories. One memory, in particular, came like a flood of warm water, enticing her mind to open to something othcr than despair. She reached over to a decanter of brandy she kept on her desk for just such an occasion. *Maybe a few sips will clear my mind. I still am not absolutely certain I'm about to do the right thing.* She took a drink, letting the brandy slip smoothly past her lips and down her throat. While it burned slightly going down, it was a satisfying tingle. The more she stared, the more she thought, and the more she thought, the more uncertain she became.

Then an idea hit her with a jolt. It would be dark in a couple of hours. She would wait for darkness to make her next move. She drank some more. The brandy seemed to sting her throat less and less as she found the bottle almost a quarter of the way down. She smiled at the thought that she could be getting drunk. She'd been sober as a judge for ten years, and it looked as if she might be about to end that run.

No, by damn. I'll not succumb to the evils of drink. She put the bottle into the safe, where she couldn't continue to sip its elixir at every whipstitch, along with replacing the deed. *If I'm to do what I have planned, I must be in my right mind and in control of all my facili—er, faculties.* She closed the door to the safe just in time. Strength of character was Molly McQueen's long suit. And she wasn't about to deviate from it now.

As darkness fell, she watched for the light to go out in Abner's office, signaling his retirement to the mess hall for a late supper and then to the bunkhouse. She watched him lock up and walk across the open yard to talk the cook into serving up some victuals, late as it was. Abner treated the cook with special care. Whenever it was time for the paychecks to be distributed, Cook always found a little something extra in his envelope. Abner assumed Molly was unaware of his little deceit, but she was fully apprised of the situation when Cook let slip that he was mighty grateful for her generosity. *A good cook can keep a company like the mine together, and I'm not about to rock the boat. Well-fed men are happy men.*

As Abner ambled to the mess hall, Molly was unlocking the door to Abner's office. She pulled a drape across the single window and lit a candle. She began poring over the ledger that covered the last year in hopes of finding somethingthat the bookkeeper had missed. She went over everything, column by column, page after page. She had to admit, Abner had handsome penmanship. But while her knowledge of accounting was quite limited, she could find nothing obviously amiss.

Finally, stretching and stifling a yawn, Molly emerged from Abner Dillard's office before he returned and slipped back into her own quarters for one more swig of brandy before she drifted off to sleep. A sleep she knew would be fitful.

Since she had found nothing amiss in the books, she was forced to return to the realization that the mine was in a mess.

I wish I'd paid the teacher more attention when she was tryin' to get me to understand all that ciphering. She patted her pillow and buried her head in it. Several tears ran down her cheeks before she nodded off.

Chapter Four

The late morning found friends Zebulan A. Pooder and Blue LeBeau trying to stare each other down across their bunks at the Gilded Lily Mine. They had been employed by the mine's new manager, Molly McQueen, ever since U.S. Marshal Piedmont Kelly had confronted the former owner, King Slaughter, accusing him of the murder of Deputy Sheriff Ben Satterfield one year back. Slaughter had chosen to draw on the marshal rather than be taken in for trial. Slaughter lost to Kelly's Winchester. Now the two boys, no longer wandering the territory in search of their next meal, were working steadily, making a decent wage, and entertaining no more worries about keeping their bellies full. At least Blue was satisfied with his lot. A seventeen-year-old from Louisiana, he'd run away from an abusive father after his mother died of a fever. Blue now had money in his pocket, a place to sleep, regular meals, and a boss lady who treated him with respect. The work wasn't easy, but he could sleep knowing it was honest work. And he no longer had nightmares about being chased all over the Territory and shot in his sleep by a gang of deranged outlaws, as he had been soon after meeting up with Pooder.

Pooder, on the other hand, was becoming more and more restless from doing the same job in the stamp mill day after day, pulling the handle, crushing the rocks. He was certain if he stayed much longer at the Lily, he'd lose his hearing altogether. He was growing increasingly anxious to move on, to find some excitement and broaden his prospects for getting rich someday. He'd regularly been going into Desert Belle on Friday nights to play poker or faro after being paid, and almost every time he'd come straggling back on Saturday morning, broke and disillusioned.

"Blue, how about you and me going into town tonight and turn a few pasteboards? What d'ya say?" Pooder said, finally having to give up any prospect of out-staring his friend. Blue could stare a hole in a rock and not blink for hours—at least that's what Pooder imagined, having never been able to last a full two minutes without his eyes beginning to water.

"Nope. I'm stayin' right here. My money doesn't need to spend any time in some gambler's pocket. No siree. I work hard for my dollars, and I intend to keep every one of 'em." Blue lay down on his bunk, laced his fingers behind his head, and closed his eyes.

"Aw, c'mon, Blue. You'll never be able to spend all that cash you got stored up. Say, I have an idea. Why don't you let me take some of your money, and I'll run it into a fortune for you? And since you're a good friend, I'll only ask a small fee for the service too."

Without opening his eyes, Blue burst out laughing. "Uh-huh. That's rich, Pooder—you making a fortune gambling. I can't recall the last time you came back with a penny in your pocket."

"I feel it comin' on. A real winnin' streak. I'm goin' to ride this one all the way. You better get in on it, or you'll be sorry. C'mon, what do you say?"

"Sorry. No sale, Pooder. I'm not sayin' you don't deserve a winning streak after all the times you've lost every cent you had to your name, but I'm not puttin' my money at risk. Besides, why would this poor boy need to go gettin' rich?"

"Why, you could buy anything you'd want. You could own a fine big house in town, up on the hill, or get yourself a black stallion to ride, instead of that worthless, white-faced mule of yours. Anything, my good man, anything you want. Think of the possibilities."

Blue had heard enough. He was tired and just wanted to take a nap. He turned his face to the wall and in no time began snoring. Pooder got up, disgusted that he hadn't been able to convince Blue to go to town with him, so he slipped his boots back on and wandered out into the

afternoon sun. He looked back at the bunkhouse
door, muttered something about Blue's being
sorry he hadn't gotten in on a sure thing, and
went to saddle his horse.

Looking up from compiling a list of items
needed from town, and seeing Pooder heading
for the corral, Molly McQueen scurried out of
the mine office and called to him.

"Where you headed, Pooder?" she shouted.

"To Desert Belle, ma'am," he answered. "That
all right?"

"Sure. Just don't be lookin' for an advance on
your pay tomorrow," she said, laughing.

Pooder hung his head. He knew he had become
the laughingstock among the other miners for his
terrible luck at gambling. For every dollar he'd
ever won, he'd lost twenty. Even he had to admit
that his luck had been running even worse of
late, but he really had become hooked on the
idea of it turning around. *A man just has to have
faith in himself,* he had said over and over to the
mocking miners.

"I'm kidding, Pooder," she said. "I want you to
take a letter to town for me. It's very important
that it get mailed today. Will you do that?"

"Why, yes, ma'am, of course," he said,
brightening at the prospect that Molly would
entrust to him an important task. Heaven
knew, smashing big rocks into little rocks was
hardly a job for a boy like eighteen-year-old Zeb

Pooder, a boy with grand dreams and schemes.

Molly handed the letter to him. He glanced at the writing on the front. It meant little to him, as his reading skills were limited, but he did appreciate the way the letters seemed to roll and ripple so rhythmically across the paper, like the lapping waters of the mighty Mississippi, the only sizable body of water he'd ever seen.

"Pooder, listen to me carefully. It's very important. This letter *must* get to the stage office before the evening coach leaves for Tucson. Make sure to give it to Mr. Baker, and tell him to put it in with the other mail. Do you understand?"

"Yes, ma'am, it's very important. You can count on me." All of a sudden Pooder seemed to stand straighter than usual, almost as if he'd enlisted in the Army or something.

"If that letter doesn't get out, we're in deep trouble. I'm putting a lot of responsibility on you, boy. Don't let me down." Molly said, and she turned quickly and strode back to the office.

"Uh, yes, ma'am," Pooder muttered to her back as she disappeared into the whipsaw-sided building. He began saddling his horse. He had stuffed the envelope into the back pocket of his jeans, since he needed both hands to get the horse ready for the long ride to town.

The afternoon sun was making the desert ripple with rising heat, and Pooder made sure to take along a full canteen of water. He'd made that ride many times and was well aware of the dangers of not being prepared. He was through making mistakes. He was determined to turn his luck around, and one way to do that was to be thorough about everything he embarked on. He'd heard from one of the older miners that sharp tools made for easier work, and he interpreted that to mean making sure you had your mind totally on the task at hand. His task, as he saw it, was to sit in at the poker table at the Shot-to-Hell Saloon in Desert Belle and win big.

Pooder kicked his mount to a run, throwing up a cloud of dust as the horse pounded through the gate. On the ground, right where he'd just thrown the old saddle onto his gray horse—the one he'd bought for two dollars from the liveryman—was an envelope half-covered in dirt.

When Pooder reached the steps of the Shot-to-Hell Saloon, he had to step aside as two cowboys came stumbling out, clinging to each other for support, singing and laughing, both as drunk as they could be. Pooder shook his head. He didn't like the taste of whiskey, so he saw no reason to spend his money gulping down the foul-tasting stuff and elected instead to save it all for the table games. He had seen too many men get roaring drunk, then lose every penny to some slick gambler who was more than willing to take their contributions into *his* bank account.

That kind of behavior was not for Zeb Pooder, no siree. He was smarter than that. Staying sober was a carefully thought out part of his plan to walk out of the saloon with a fistful of cash. He had walked in intent on winning, and, by damn, win he would. He threw his shoulders back and strode through the bat-wing doors with confidence. He immediately spotted three cowboys with whom he'd played cards before on several occasions, sitting at a table in a corner. A fourth chair was empty. That looked to him like as good a spot as any to begin his quest. A half-empty bottle of whiskey sat on the table, along with three glasses. That was a good sign. He figured if they were already on their way to being drunk, he'd stand an even better chance of taking their wages away from them. He walked over.

"Howdy, gents. Mind if I sit in?"

One of them, a scruffy, ruddy-faced man with a beat-up old slouch hat who had been shuffling the deck, looked up and said, "You think you can keep up, Pooder?"

"Yes, sir, today I think I can. In fact, I hope you fellas are well heeled, because I feel lucky tonight, real lucky."

"We like a boy who feels lucky, don't we, gents?" the man said with a grin. The others nodded as Pooder sat down. Another man wandered up and pulled over another chair.

"Got room for one more?" he said.

"Glad to have you. We're the Clutter brothers —Bob, Joe and me, I'm Hank. What's your handle?"

"Wimberley. And who is this young man?"

"Zebulan Pooder, from Ohio."

"Zebulan? What the hell kind of name is that?"

Zeb's faced turned red as he said, "Uh, most folks just call me Pooder."

"Well, all right, *Pooder*. That's just what I'll do too."

"Pooder, you want to cut for deal?" Hank said.

"Okay." Pooder cut the deck, turned over an ace, and Hank pushed all the cards toward him.

"Let's get at 'er, boy," said Hank.

Pooder peeled off the cards. Hank began rolling a cigarette.

An hour later, Pooder was down to his last four dollars. Wimberley wasn't faring any better. The Clutter brothers, getting drunker by the minute, had all but cleaned them out. Pooder couldn't understand how it could happen. His plan was crumbling before his eyes. He bowed his head in disgust. That's when he spotted it on the floor, by Hank's left boot. It was the ace of spades. How'd that get on the floor?

He wasn't quite sure what to do or say. Clearly, you couldn't play a fair game without all fifty-two pasteboards, but he didn't have a gun. Besides, calling these three out might just be a fatal mistake. Maybe it had dropped by accident, he rationalized. But thinking back on the last hand Bob had held and won the pot with, he'd had four aces. How could he have done that if one of them was on the floor? Pooder knew he had to leave the game and get out of there quickly, maybe go tell the sheriff that there was illegal gambling going on in the saloon. But then, he really couldn't prove such an accusation, and the Clutters might just take it into their minds to kill him for suggesting they were cheats. But he had to do something, and right away, or face another jeering from the other miners for his inability to recognize that poker might not be for him. Just then Wimberley pushed his chair back and got up. He walked toward the door without a word.

"Gents, I reckon I've had enough for tonight. I think I'll head on back to the Gilded Lily and get some sleep before tomorrow," Pooder said, scooting his chair back.

The three Clutters looked at him as if he'd just kicked mud onto their new Sunday-go-to-meeting boots.

"You sure you want to do that, sonny?" Hank said. "We ain't ready to leave."

"I, uh, don't want to spoil your game, but I really gotta go." Pooder stood and started to leave. He was grabbed by the arm and pulled back. When he turned, it was Bob Clutter who had him and was yanking him back into his chair.

"Nobody leaves a game until we say so. So sit down and finish what you started."

"Wh-What about Wimberley?"

"We ain't holdin' no IOUs from him."

Pooder was shaking so hard, he could hardly focus on the five cards he'd just been dealt. *Great, another losing hand.*

Chapter Five

Blue LeBeau had finished his chores and was on his way to the equipment barn to return the hammer and nails he'd used to crate up some broken equipment. He was passing the corral with his head down when something white seemed briefly to flutter in the breeze. It was sticking out of the dirt. He bent down and pulled an envelope free from where it looked like a horse's hooves had stomped on it and nearly buried it. He wiped it clean so he could read whatever was written on one side. It appeared to be a letter, and it was addressed to someone in Tucson, and sent by Molly McQueen, Manager of the Gilded Lily Mine. Blue's eyes grew wide as he saw how official the envelope looked. *What the devil is this doing out here in the middle of nowhere?* He ran to the office to find Molly.

When he burst through the door, he was greeted by a look of surprise on the face of Abner Dillard, the bookkeeper. Abner's expression quickly turned to disgust at recognizing who had entered so rudely.

"Blue LeBeau, what in tarnation would possess a boy to crash through the door to a proper office without so much as a knock? Didn't nobody teach you any manners down in them backward bayous where you was spawned?"

"Uh, yessir, I think they did, sir, uh, whatever it was you said. Sorry for making so much racket, but I need—"

"*You* need? It's always what you young rapscallions need, isn't it? Never stopping to think about what others need. I swear, I cannot fathom whatever possessed a sensible, hard-workin' woman like Molly McQueen to hire on you two no-accounts. Now, you either git your-self out of here and don't come back until you can enter proper, or don't come back at all. You understand? Now, shoo."

"But, Mr. Abner, it's important that I—"

"Ain't nothin' so important that you can't act civilized, young man. Now git."

"But, sir, I—"

"Git!" Abner Dillard had slid off his stool and raised himself up to his full height, that of about five and a half feet. He puffed out his scrawny chest and pointed a finger straight at the dis-concerted boy. Several spots of ink dotted Abner's white shirt and wide red suspenders, the result of his being startled by Blue's untimely entrance. Dillard hadn't yet noticed the inky blemishes, for if he had, his temper would have certainly exploded into near apoplexy.

Blue left the office in such a hurry, he forgot

to pull the door shut behind him, resulting in another shouted condemnation from the flustered bookkeeper. Blue didn't look back as he went elsewhere to locate Molly.

His steps led him first to the corral, then to the mill. He found neither Molly nor anyone who had seen her since before noon. Blue hung his head and pondered his next move. While he hadn't any idea of what might be contained in the envelope he clutched in his sweaty hand, he had a strong feeling it was all-fired important and that he'd better waste no time in finding Molly or else.

Suddenly, his silent prayers were answered as he looked up to see Molly coming out of the tent of the doctor. She was wiping her hands on what appeared to be a bloodstained towel, and the look on her face was one of worry.

"Miz Molly, ma'am, I-I need to see you, if'n that's all right," Blue stammered, and he yanked his hat from his head.

For some reason or another, he found talking one-on-one with the manager of the mine something that a runaway boy from Louisiana shouldn't do. Molly, on the other hand, had never implied that she was any more important than any of the twenty men who worked the Gilded Lily Mine.

"Of course, Blue. Come into my office. I must wash this blood off my hands. It looks like we've lost a good man, at least for several weeks.

Johnny Benson fell in front of the tram and nearly lost his arm. The doc thinks he can save it, but Johnny won't be returning to work for quite a while."

"Gosh, that's awful. I reckon I'm glad I don't work down there. I'm sorta clumsy, especially around mechanical things."

Molly nodded as she poured water into a basin and began scrubbing her hands with lye soap. When she had dried off, she sat at her desk and smiled at Blue.

"Now, young man, what can I do for you?"

Blue pulled the wrinkled envelope from his pants pocket and thrust it toward her. "I, uh, found this out by the corral, in the dirt, and it looked important."

Molly's eyes grew wide at the sight of the letter she had entrusted to the care of Zeb Pooder. Her face grew dark. The promise he'd given to guard it with his life, seeing to it that it was handed over safe and sound into the hands of the postmaster in Desert Belle, had been worthless.

She slumped in her chair. Her expression turned dour. Blue thought he might have even seen a tear start to form in the corner of one eye.

"I'm goin' to kill that irresponsible pig farmer! Wait'll I get my hands on him."

"Sounds like this letter is mighty important."

"It *is* important. It's a matter of the Lily's staying in business or not."

Molly went on to explain that if the envelope didn't get to Tucson in a couple of days, the mine could go into foreclosure, something she had just found out from the mine's bookkeeper.

"But I thought everything was going so well. We're takin' gold outta here, aren't we? That's what I thought I've been bustin' my back doin' this livelong year," Blue said through gritted teeth.

"That's what I thought too, but recently Abner says our assets are dwindling. He says we're taking too much cash out of the place. And that's what's got me worried. I'm the only one who can make withdrawals, and I haven't made any for more'n two months. The only thing going out is payroll and supplies for the mess hall."

"Could someone be stealing money?" Blue asked.

"I don't see how," Molly said, nearly in tears. "It looks particularly bad for me, since I'm the only one who can write checks for payroll."

"Damn," Blue muttered.

"We are lost" was all she could say, and that caught in her throat as she looked away and shook her head.

"Is there anything I can do?"

Molly sat for several minutes without saying a word; then she sighed.

"I told Pooder how important it was that this letter get out in today's mail. He obviously was more interested in getting back to his card games than to making sure the mine survives. How could anyone be that irresponsible?"

"I-I could saddle up and try to get it to town. Give me a chance, will you? I sure don't want anything to happen to the mine, or to you either." Blue began wringing his hands. This was the first job he'd ever had where he actually got paid, even if it was backbreaking work, and he didn't want to lose it.

Molly managed a weak smile. "I know you don't, Blue. You're a good, hardworking lad. I'm proud to have you working here, but it'll take more than hard work to save us now. It'll take a miracle."

"Won't you at least let me try, ma'am? I'd consider it an honor."

Molly began thinking about Blue's proposition. It was the middle of the afternoon, and the stage for Tucson was scheduled to leave at 4:30. If he took the fastest horse the mine owned, it would take him two and a half hours, and that was if nothing got in his way to slow him down. But maybe it was worth a try. She jumped up, waved the letter at him, and, as he took it, her eyes narrowed.

"Blue, this may be the most important thing you've ever been asked to do in your life. Many men's jobs are on the line here. If this doesn't get to Tucson by Monday, the mine could lose everything. Do you understand the importance of what I'm asking you to do?"

"Yes, ma'am. You can count on me."

Molly went to the door and shouted toward the corral. "Charlie, saddle up Quicksilver, and don't waste no time about it."

She turned to Blue with a stern look. "You hand this to the postmaster and only to the postmaster. Don't stop for anything. Make sure he understands how important it is that it gets to Tucson. Any questions?"

"No, ma'am," Blue said as he flew from the porch, landing on the dusty ground at a dead run toward the corral, where Charlie was saddling the fleetest horse they had. He felt an enormous amount of pride that Molly had given him this chance to prove himself more valuable to the Gilded Lily than as just a handyman and gofer. He folded the envelope, slipped it into his shirt pocket, then pulled his handkerchief from his back pocket and stuffed that in on top of the letter, just to make sure it didn't come loose from being jostled around while he was in the saddle.

Charlie was tightening the latigo when Blue started to climb on. He was wasting no time in getting on with the task at hand. Henry stepped back, and Blue slapped the reins with a loud *crack*. The dapple-gray mare leaped at the boy's command and burst out of the corral at a full gallop. No more than a quarter of a mile down the road, Blue's floppy hat left his head and went sailing off into the cactus. He would try to

50

retrieve it on his way back, but not now. There were more important things to attend to. His future at his first real job was at stake.

Pooder was in a near panic. He'd gotten himself into ticklish situations before, but never one where he saw no way out. The odds were stacked against him this time as they'd never been before. *Why did he get himself into such scrapes, anyway?* he wondered.

Just then, he remembered the envelope from Molly. That would be just the excuse he needed to escape these misfits who were trying their best to relieve him of every last penny.

"Gentlemen, I'm afraid I must leave you, if only for a brief time, in order to deliver an important letter to the postmaster from the boss lady at the Gilded Lily." He gave a big grin as he reached around, fully expecting to feel the envelope snugly tucked away in his hip pocket.

Now was the time for real panic to set in. The envelope was gone. He fumbled around, patting each pocket several times, trying to convince himself that he'd just forgotten which pocket he had put it into. His face was flushed with fear. Perspiration poured off his brow, and his hands began shaking. "I'm dead, truly and deservedly dead," he muttered.

"What'd you say, Pooder?" Hank asked.

"I—er . . ."

"Quit mumblin', boy. What's all this nonsense about an envelope? Where is it, anyway? I'm thinkin' this is one of your tricks to get us to let you leave the table and get out of playin' to the very end," Hank said, a sneer on his twisted mouth. He pulled his six-shooter and placed it on the table. Joe and Bob both leaned forward on their elbows. "Of course, you wouldn't try a foolish trick like that on us upstandin' citizens, would you?"

If Pooder could have crawled into a knothole, he wouldn't have hesitated at that moment. Here he was, faced with severe consequences at either turn. Molly would kill him for losing the letter, and these gunslingers would use him for target practice if he tried to leave the game. Zebulan A. Pooder, late of an Ohio pig farm, was doomed, plain and simple. And the worst of it was, he knew it and could do nothing to stop his world from crumbling right before his eyes.

In for a penny, in for a pound, he remembered his drunken father saying every time his mother berated the man for coming home so drunk he could hardly stand. But it was a phrase that had stuck with the young boy, and this was as good a time as any to use it. He stood up suddenly, reached into his pants pocket, and pulled out his last two dollars. He threw the money onto the table in front of the others.

"Here, take it. I ain't got no more. You cleaned

me out. Now I have to find that envelope," Pooder said, as he turned and stormed toward the door. *I ain't heard no gunshot, so this might just work,* he thought.

His pulse was racing by the time he reached the swinging doors. Within seconds, however, any hope of escape was dashed when he heard heavy footsteps closing behind him quickly and the sinister voice of Hank Clutter saying, "We'll just go along with you, boy. Maybe there'll be some money in it."

If I live through this day, I swear I'll never sit down at a gambling table again so long as I live. I swear, I swear, I swear, Pooder said over and over in his head. As badly as he was perspiring, one might have thought he'd come in out of a thunderstorm.

Chapter Six

U.S. Marshal Piedmont Kelly leaned on his saddle horn and surveyed the scene that lay before him: the vast, empty desert north of Bisbee, from where he'd just come. He had been called there to solve a series of murders of miners. It hadn't taken long. It had been clear from the start who the killer was because the man responsible had bothered neither to cover his tracks nor hide his identity. A propensity for overindulging in rotgut whiskey, a loose mouth, and a mule whose tracks a child could follow had made Kelly's trip south more like a vacation than work. Kelly had left Bisbee after a week, with one man in the county lockup and a trail of death fueled by greed uncovered. It was back to Cochise for a comfortable bed and some of Nettie's good victuals.

As he rode, he reminisced about the last time he'd been in Cochise, about the friendship of Sheriff Stevens, and his growing feelings for the lady who owned the best eating-place in a hundred miles. He wasn't quite sure what to call it, but he had to entertain the thought that what he felt for Nettie could be akin to love—or whatever all those poets down through the ages had referred to as love. Since he'd only had feelings so strong for one woman before, the whole thing was still something of a puzzle.

And what of Nettie? What woman would let herself get emotionally involved with a lawman, someone who risks his life every time he straps on a gun and steps outside? He had to consider both sides of the issue. Just because he had feelings that seemed to grow more intense each time he thought about her, that didn't mean she felt the same or that she had any intention of a deeper involvement. *Maybe she just wants a friendship, an easygoing, no-pressure kind of relationship that puts no demands on either of us. Have I pushed too hard? Should I let her know how I feel, or just let things take their natural course?* His mental meanderings almost caused him to miss the turnoff to Cochise ten miles out.

When he finally arrived in town a couple of hours later, he decided to check in with Sheriff John Henry Stevens first. He needed to get his mind off Nettie long enough to give him a break from uncertainty and put his romantic quandary aside for a spell. He dismounted in front of the jail. Stevens stepped onto the boardwalk as Kelly was draping his horse's reins over the railing.

"I'm glad to see you, Marshal. Come inside, and let's chat over some coffee. I could use your opinion on something."

"Your looking for advice is sorta like the town

drunk bein' eager for a bath." Kelly stomped his boots on the boards and followed Stevens inside. The sheriff's response to Kelly's comment was nothing more than a grunt.

Handing Kelly a cup of coffee, Stevens said, "Seat yourself and have a listen, will you? And maybe lay off the hints at my bein' a stubborn old fool."

Kelly laughed. "Okay, John Henry, but I didn't actually mean to imply—"

"Yeah, yeah, I know. Just listen up for a minute, will you? There were three strangers in town yesterday. They smelled like bounty hunters. Said they were lookin' for a man named Alex Bowdre. The bartender told 'em the only Alex he'd heard of was Alex Bond, a man who has a small spread north of town a few miles. They rode out that way, talkin' about takin' a look at the fella. I'm of the opinion that one of them could be Snake Torres."

"Hmm. What would they find when they got there? Any indication this Bond is the man they're lookin' for?"

"Don't know. They haven't been back."

"What's this Bowdre fella wanted for? Did you look him up?"

"Yeah. First off they said he was Charlie Bowdre's brother—you know, the one who was known to be ridin' with that young hellion Billy Bonney."

"Billy the Kid?"

"The one and only. The kid that got himself embroiled in that war of sorts over in New Mexico. They say that youngster's killed twenty men. Did you know that? Hard to believe."

"Yep, mighty hard. But you didn't say whether you found a dodger on Alex Bond or Bowdre, whichever it turns out to be."

"I did and I didn't. Here's the situation. I finally found some paper on Alex Bowdre, wanted for rustlin'. Had his picture on it too. I didn't recognize him. I've only seen this Bond fella once, and from quite a distance. He came into town for supplies, then scooted out like he didn't want nothin' to do with townfolk. But I'd have to say, it ain't likely he's the same man."

"So what's the advice you're lookin' to me for?"

"I was thinkin' maybe you'd want to take a ride out to the Bond place with me, kinda look the situation over. Wouldn't mind puttin' my mind at ease about what them bounty hunters might be up to."

"I don't suppose you could wait till I get a bite to eat before climbin' back into that saddle."

"It ain't food you're eager for, Piedmont Kelly. I'm a bit past my prime, but I ain't no confounded idjit, neither," Stevens said. "You don't fool me. Go on over there and visit your lady friend. I'll just be here twiddlin' my thumbs till you get back."

Kelly left with a wide grin on his face. He walked across the street to Nettie's little restaurant. A bell tinkled when he opened the door. He looked around and found the place empty, likely since it was the middle of the afternoon, too late for lunch and too early for supper. Nettie was wiping her hands as she popped through the curtain separating the kitchen from the dining room. The expression on her face was pleasant but didn't show any eagerness for another mouth to feed in the middle of the day. When she saw Kelly, that all changed.

"Piedmont! Oh, I'm so glad you're back, safe and sound." She rushed to him and threw her arms around his neck. He was almost thrown off balance by her exuberance. He recovered quickly as his arms slid around her slim waist. The feel of her near him sent a charge through him like touching a bare telegraph wire. They hugged for a minute before she pulled back, took him by the hand, and guided him to a table.

"I'll bet you're starved after being on that dusty road for so long. I have just the thing to make a saddle-weary marshal happy." She started to turn away and head into the kitchen when Kelly grabbed her arm and pulled her back. He pulled her close and kissed her.

"*That's* what makes this weary marshal happy."

His words brought a sudden sparkle to her eyes. At first she seemed surprised, but as she stepped back slowly, a shy smile crossed her lips. She twirled around and went through the curtains like a little girl who'd just been given a piece of sweet candy.

It took Kelly and the sheriff only about two hours to reach the Bond spread. When they reached the gate, about fifteen yards from the front of the small, clapboard-sided bungalow, Kelly called out.

"Mr. Bond, it's Sheriff Stevens and Marshal Kelly. Are you home?"

The wind blew only the sounds of birds to his ears. No answer from Bond. He dismounted, pushed through the gate, and stepped carefully onto the porch. He called out again and again received no answer.

"John Henry, why don't you go around back and see if he might be in the barn or fetchin' water from the well?"

The sheriff nudged his horse around to the back, where an ocotillo corral had been constructed and a rough barn of sorts stood with the doors wide open. There were no horses in either place. In fact, he saw no livestock of any sort. He dismounted, let his horse drink from the trough, and went to join the marshal in the house. Sensing water, Piedmont's black gelding made his way around to the watering trough as well.

"See any signs out back that might indicate what happened here?" Kelly said.

"Nothing. No horses, chickens, pigs, cattle, sheep—nothing."

Just then Kelly spied what looked like blood on the floor. He bent over to more closely examine several dried splotches. He went back outside and stood with his arms crossed.

"What are you thinkin', Marshal?"

"I'm trying to decide how three men, intent on sneakin' up on a man to capture him, might go about such a deed. There's not much cover out there. The yard is wide, and there's only those few boulders over there to get behind. Several trees, but none really substantial."

"That's what I was thinkin' too. So, if they got the drop on him, just how'd they go about it? Other than pepperin' the front door with bullets, which it appears they did."

"Let's look around and see if there's any evidence that points to this Bond fella bein' wanted for anything," Kelly said. "Or that he might indeed be this Bowdre."

He walked to a rolltop desk and pulled on the handle. It rolled open to reveal a ledger and caches of correspondence from all over. He pulled a handful out of one of the cubicles and handed it to Stevens, taking another for himself. He sat in the swiveling captain's chair, while Stevens got comfortable in a leather wingback.

Kelly read several letters, then opened the ledger. Inside he found that the man calling himself Bond was a businessman who invested in failing companies, built them back to profitability, then sold them at an even higher profit.

"This fella's doin' all right for himself, John Henry. He doesn't need to be rustlin' cattle; he's already wealthy."

"Yeah. This piece of paper says he just sold a thousand-acre ranch in Texas to a fella for about twice what he paid for it. And it all took place within a year."

"Hmm, now here's one that's interesting. He got somethin' back from an inquiry about a mine over in Desert Belle."

"What mine is it? Don't you know some folks over there?"

"I sure do, and the mine he's talking about is the Gilded Lily. Molly McQueen is running the operation. Last I heard, she was doing well, and the mine was showing a healthy profit," Kelly said. He began stroking his chin, deep in thought. He replaced the stack of papers in the desk cubicle and got up and walked to the window. He parted the curtain and stared out at the deserted land.

"What're you thinkin', Marshal?"

"I'm thinkin' those bounty hunters have the wrong man. I'm also thinkin' we need to find them before they do something they could get themselves strung up for."

"I reckon that's the right thing to do, but—"

"But what, John Henry?" Kelly turned to give the sheriff a puzzled look. "Is there somethin' you disagree with?"

"Don't disagree at all, but I can't go along with you. I'm due back in town in the mornin' for an important town meetin', and if I'm not there, they might just up and get a new sheriff by default. Sorta a command performance, if you see what I mean."

"They can't kick you out of a job that you were duly elected to, can they?"

"This new bunch that's runnin' things sorta follow their own agenda, I'm afraid. Talk is, they'd like nothing better than to find some young stallion who'd do their bidding without any questions. And you know I ain't that sort. I been a lawman too long to get run over by a stampede of saloon owners who'd like to see the rules eased a mite for the cowboys when it comes to wearin' guns in town and hurrah-in' the honest, law-abidin' folks, shootin' out windows, and the like."

"Got you with your back to the wall, sounds like. Well, never you mind. I'll go after the bounty hunters, and you get back and straighten out your council. When I return, we'll see what can be done about quietin' things down a mite. That suit you, John Henry?"

"Suits me fine."

"When you get a chance, would you telegraph

the Indian Agent up in San Carlos and ask if he would send that Apache scout, Spotted Dog, to meet me at Ambush Creek? He'll know where. Tell him to be there day after tomorrow by noon."

"That's the same Injun that Drago shot and whose life you saved, ain't he?"

"That's him. Good man too."

"And to think I near let him get tried for a crime he didn't commit," Stevens said.

"I'm real glad you didn't."

The sheriff nodded his agreement as he got mounted. They both wheeled their horses about and rode out in different directions, each with a problem to solve, and each up against superior odds.

Chapter Seven

Marshal Kelly certainly wasn't looking forward to tracking three bounty hunters to hell and back through the hot desert sand. He had no idea whether they had Alex Bond with them and, if so, whether he was dead or alive. He also couldn't fathom why—when Cochise had a sheriff and it was only ten miles to the south—they would head into the blistering furnace to the northwest, with no towns of consequence for fifty miles. It made no sense if their intention really was to turn Bond over to the law and collect a reward— assuming he was wanted for something.

As the sun dipped toward the mountains to the west, he came to a tiny spring burbling from the base of some boulders and struggling to keep a pool full before the water evaporated. Several trees and some wildflowers were taking advantage of the gift of life, as tenuous as it was. This insignificant oasis was the only such refuge for miles around. *This looks like a good place to camp.* He dismounted, hobbled his black gelding, and tossed his saddle against the trunk of the single tree he deemed sufficiently substantial to lean against. He was able to gather enough deadfall from nearby trees to build a fire for some coffee and a plateful of beans. It wouldn't keep him warm when the night began to cool down, however, so he unrolled his blankets and threw them down next to his saddle.

He pulled his canteens off the saddle horn, unscrewed the caps, and knelt down beside the spring to refill them. Just as he was about to dip one into the cool water, he was met with a strange smell. He stopped and bent down closer to the water. The smell was of something foul—a chemical odor rather than a dead animal. He got up, recapped the still partly full canteens, and began a search around the periphery of the watering hole. Several yards away he found a couple of rabbits and, farther yet, a coyote lying dead, facing away from the water. They'd died quickly and painfully. Fortunately, Kelly's horse had gone straight for a mat of grass that had taken hold beneath a rocky overhang where shade was plentiful and had shunned the water—temporarily, at least.

Someone has committed the worst sin a man can commit in the desert: He's poisoned a water hole and, in doing so, has condemned possibly hundreds of living creatures to death. He was able to identify tracks left around the area as those he'd been following for much of the day. Four horses. The bounty hunters were taking precautions to prevent anyone from following them. *Desperate men do desperate things,* he thought. It was clear these particular men weren't who Sheriff Stevens thought they were and were up to something more devious than a simple fugitive capture for reward.

Kelly knew that trying to do something about the poisoned water would put him farther behind his quarry, but he couldn't leave things as they were. Since the spring itself likely hadn't been tainted, he set out to change the course of the water flow. With a folding shovel from his saddlebags, he began scraping a new channel so the water would flow away from the pool of deadly toxin. When he had several feet cleared, he began tossing dirt into the existing pool in an attempt to dry up the poisoned water. He filled his hat with water straight from the spring and held it out to his gelding. The horse slurped it noisily. He tilted his canteens to direct the flow into them. When he felt certain he had enough water to get him to the creek where he was to meet Spotted Dog, he again set out following the four horsemen, changing his mind about camping in this location. He decided it best to continue on to his rendezvous point with the Indian.

The tracks seemed to be taking a strange course. They weren't headed straight for Tombstone or Tucson or Fort Huachuca—any of the obvious places to turn a man over to authorities to collect a bounty—*if* there was a bounty on this man, which the marshal had begun to doubt more and more. The tracks headed for a mountain range to the west. That was okay with Kelly because they would lead him in the right direction to meet up with Spotted Dog, the old Chiricahua Apache scout whose life he'd saved only months earlier. He looked forward to again seeing this man he'd befriended, having found him trustworthy and honorable. The place he'd asked Sheriff Stevens to instruct the Indian to meet him was only a few miles off the course the bounty hunters appeared to be taking.

It was early evening when he rode into sight of the wash with a small stream running through the middle called Ambush Creek. It wasn't hard to figure out where the name came from. Trees and boulders lined the sides of the wash—plenty of places to hide in wait for the unwary to approach the stream to water their horses or cattle. Tales concocted by overactive imaginations —of murderous thieves and Apache renegades attacking travelers, killing and plundering them of all their earthly goods and leaving their bodies to bleach white in the sun—came and went like dust devils. While he discounted those stories as nothing but ammunition of those for whom tall tales had become a way of life, the place held a fascination for him, nevertheless. The true story was enough to chill a man to the bone, giving the wary pause to reconsider stopping here.

Off in the distance, he saw a pinto pony grazing alongside the stream, although he had yet to see Spotted Dog. As he got closer, the old Indian stepped out from behind a boulder, carrying his Spencer rifle across his chest, one hand raised in greeting. Kelly dismounted and turned his gelding loose to find water.

"It is good to see you, Spotted Dog." He reached out a hand, which the Indian took with a strong grip.

"And you, my friend. You have work for me?"

"Indeed. I want to take advantage of your fine tracking skills. I've been trying to follow three bounty hunters and their captive. Did you happen to see anyone pass this way in the last few hours?"

"I see no one. What of the men you follow?"

"The man they are holding may not be wanted at all. I must catch up to them before they do something they might regret."

"We start now?"

"I reckon we might as well, while there is still plenty of light. We may be able to reach the base of those hills before having to make camp."

Spotted Dog nodded and swung onto the pony's back. He rode with only a thick blanket on his mount. When last Kelly had seen him, the Indian had been without a horse and was forced to ride a mare whose owner had been murdered in Kelly's camp. That horse and its saddle were clearly not what the Indian would have chosen to ride if he'd had a voice in the matter.

Kelly pointed Spotted Dog in the general direction of where he'd last seen the bounty hunters' tracks. The Indian rode off ahead, zigzagging right and left to make certain of cutting the trail as quickly as possible. The marshal could tell by Spotted Dog's posture that he was happy to be serving some useful purpose, rather than sitting around a fire with the other old men on the reservation. Kelly had great empathy for the old Apache, holding him in high esteem as a man whose skills at survival in the desert were second to none. He also enjoyed the man's quiet demeanor and poise. He had no idea what this Indian's life had been like before coming across him in the desert, wounded and near death. In saving his life, he'd made a faithful friend forever.

"Four horses head for mountain, there," Spotted Dog said, pointing the way.

"Good. Perhaps we'll catch up to them soon."

"Maybe not find what you think."

"What do you mean?"

"Might be three dead men. Only one alive."

"How can you tell a thing like that?"

"Tracks follow in line, not spread out. One leading other three horses in trail."

"You mean like they are tied one to the other?"

"Think so."

"What else can you tell me about these four?

69

And what makes you think three are dead?"

"Hoofprints not change. Weight they carry not shift side to side—dead weight. Only lead horse show change in way he walk."

"If it's true what you say, and we don't know who, or what, we're tracking, the sooner we catch up to them, the better. Are they keeping up a steady pace?"

"Not in hurry."

"Good. Maybe he's only guessing there might be someone trailing him. I don't want to push our mounts too hard, since water is scarce around here. The one watering hole I came upon had been deliberately poisoned. Whoever is in the lead of this bunch must know he can't travel too fast. That's probably why he tainted that pool, to slow down anyone who *might* be following him."

"Still dangerous."

"You are correct. Whoever is leading those horses is likely damned desperate. And I still don't know why, or even who he is."

It was twilight when Kelly and Spotted Dog reached the foothills and began looking for a decent place to camp. The bounty hunters' trail had led to the mouth of a narrow canyon that split the mountain like a meandering stream.

"Tracks lead into place of snake spirit," Spotted Dog said.

"We'll camp here tonight and go in after them in the morning. I'll pull out some coffee and beans."

"Spotted Dog gather wood for fire." The Apache turned and sprinted off without waiting for a reply from Kelly.

By the time he returned with an armload of dead mesquite branches, the marshal had opened a can of beans and had poured water into the coffeepot along with a handful of coffee straight from the Arbuckle's bag. Kelly struck a Lucifer and had a good fire going in minutes. By dark, they had finished and were settling in for the night.

"I'm glad you were able to join me, Spotted Dog. Thank you."

"No need thank me. I am happy to escape old men who sit around and talk of better days. Those days gone. No one looks to tomorrow. Old days only good for telling stories to children."

Kelly found himself smiling at the old Apache's complaining. He fully understood that recounting one's past wasn't always pleasant, and all memories weren't good. The loss of his own father to a gang of bank robbers was what had set him on a course to becoming a lawman, intent on seeing to it that vicious men were punished for their evil deeds. That event had convinced Kelly that there was another way to see justice done, other than being a preacher as his father was.

"I reckon I'd have to agree with you, Spotted Dog. A man can't change the past; he can only have a say in what happens tomorrow."

"Sitting with old men can't change anything.

Need purpose in life. You rescue me from old men and give me purpose."

Kelly leaned back against his saddle with a knowing smile, crossed his arms, and got lost in watching the embers slowly die out. He drank the last few sips of coffee, then scooted down and pulled a blanket over him. Spotted Dog wrapped his blanket around his shoulders and slumped against a boulder. They were both asleep in minutes.

The next morning, soon after dawn, as Kelly and Spotted Dog prepared to continue the chase, a thundering explosion from deep inside the canyon greeted them. Dust and smoke belched out of the narrow gap and briefly engulfed them in a cloud of debris.

"Looks as if someone doesn't want us following his trail anymore. We may have no choice but to go around the base of the mountain if, as I suspect, that blast closed off the pass." He slapped at his shirt and pants to remove the dust.

"I will ride into belly of mountain to see. You wait," Spotted Dog said, swinging his leg over the back of his pony.

"Nothin' doing. I'm not sending you in there alone. He may have another surprise for us. Two sets of eyes will be better than one. Let's go." Pulling his Winchester from the saddle scabbard, Kelly led the way into the slowly settling cloud of dust.

Chapter Eight

A half mile into the jaws of the canyon, the two quickly verified the impassable scene that lay before them. Kelly dismounted as Spotted Dog began searching for tracks that might suggest someone could still be lurking nearby and that the danger to them was not past.

"Tracks lead straight into rocks."

"That means he stopped to set the charge, then made his escape through the other side. We have no choice but to go back and find another route."

Spotted Dog didn't move. He stared at the mound of rubble for a minute, then turned to the marshal. "I climb over. You take pony and find trail to other side. I join you there."

Kelly rubbed his chin for a moment, recognizing that Spotted Dog's idea was sound. But he was also aware of the danger that might lie just on the other side of all those boulders. The bounty hunter, or whomever it was that Kelly was trailing, could easily be lying in wait for just such an attempt to catch him unaware.

"Be damned careful, Spotted Dog. He could be hunkered down in the rocks on the other side, and you'd be an easy target. If I remember right, this cut should continue on for about a mile. As soon as I find a way up and over the ridge to the other end, I'll ride back toward the source of the explosion and meet you. If we're lucky, we might catch him in the middle."

"That good plan," Spotted Dog said, and he sprinted up the pile of rubble like a mountain goat. Kelly just shook his head. *I must be crazy to worry about the welfare of an Apache.*

For a moment, he gazed at the pile of rubble left by the explosion. Various colors of rock—sandstone, quartz, granite, copper ore—all melded into a useless mound, looking like tailings from a mining operation over which still hung a thin cloud of fine dust. He wheeled his gelding around and started backtracking through the narrow gorge. In a few minutes, he arrived at the camp they'd made the night before, then turned south to find an alternate route over the mountain. He soon came to a trail used by mule deer that appeared to lead straight to the top. He urged his mount up the incline, leading Spotted Dog's pony. *If this goes where I think it might, I can ride the spine of the mountain all the way to the other end.*

The trail was quite narrow, and one misstep could send rider and horses hurtling over the side of the mountain to their deaths. He reined the gelding to a halt, then dismounted, choosing to take no chances. He tied the horses together in-line, taking his gelding by the reins and walking him gingerly along the here-and-there trail. He could only hope that in doing so, he would add a sufficient margin of safety. As he walked, he puzzled over a question that had come to him when they found the passage blocked: *Who in his right mind sets off on a journey through such treacherous country in blistering heat carrying dynamite on horseback? Someone intent on using it from the start of the journey, I'll wager. All of which makes one thing certain: This whole thing was well planned out.*

But he had no idea who the planner might be. He really knew none of the players in this intrigue. *I wish John Henry hadn't turned back. I could use whatever knowledge he has of these men right about now.* Just then, he noticed the trail begin to descend, winding around and through the scrub pine, causing him to lead the horses precariously close to the precipitous drop-off. He continued to lead the horses rather than take a chance on a misstep on the rocky slope. When he came to a clearing, he could see the cut below dissolve into a broad valley. There was no one in sight. As he reached the bottom, he mounted up and began leading Spotted Dog's pony back toward where he expected to find the Indian waiting. Several minutes of riding brought him to the opposite pile of rocky destruction, but there was no sight of the Apache, only acres and acres of cacti and brittlebush.

He tied the two mounts to a nearby branch of a crooked juniper that grew defiantly from a split in some boulders, gave the branch a tug to assure it would stay put, then began the trek to the top of the pile of rubble. He called out to the Apache but got no response. He looked around for evidence to indicate that the old man had made it safely over the huge pile of rocks. Seeing nothing, he turned to make certain the horses were still secured before setting out to search for Spotted Dog. He no sooner reached his black gelding than he heard a voice calling him. He looked around to see the Indian descending the steep side of the cut.

"I am here. I find something."

Kelly met Spotted Dog at a spot where the Indian had been surveying the trail ahead.

"What is it? What have you found?"

"Tracks lead away from here to valley."

"So, they *did* blow up the side of the mountain to stop us from pursuing them." Kelly rubbed at his chin, a scowl crawling across his weathered face.

"Don't think so. Think man who make explosion make grave for companions."

"Are you saying there are dead bodies under this pile of rubble? Any idea how many?"

"I think three spirits dwell here forever."

"How do you know this? And what of the horses?"

"Four sets of tracks ride away, that direction.

Only one rider. Other three horses still being led. No riders." The Apache pointed off toward a range of purple mountains across a wide valley.

"The other three couldn't have left their horses and escaped over the mountain?"

"Where we stand is the smell of death. Do you not know this?"

"I, uh, reckon I don't have the nose for such things. Okay, we'll head out after the one remaining man. No sense hangin' around a grave. I sure don't aim to try digging up the evidence."

They mounted up and began the task of tracking the remaining man, a man who held nothing but mystery to Kelly. He was deep in thought when Spotted Dog squinted at him. Kelly noticed his questioning glance.

"I know what you're wondering, and, no, I have no idea who we are tracking. I started out looking for four men, and now I'm down to one. And that one could be one of the bounty hunters or it could be the rancher, Alex Bond. Even if I came face-to-face with the man, I wouldn't know him. Never laid eyes on any of 'em."

"Know where he go?"

"Nope, but he seems to be making a beeline for someplace in particular. He don't seem to be wandering around out here with no purpose. And with three other horses to take turns riding, he can make good time."

"You right. He now travel faster."

• • •

Late afternoon brought Marshal Kelly and Spotted Dog to the crest of a mountain pass that looked down on a vast expanse of desert and not much else. Kelly pulled his field glasses from his saddlebags and began scanning for signs of their quarry. After staring through the undulating waves of heat rising from the floor of the desert, he picked up a cloud of dust traveling fast to the southwest.

"Looks like that could be our man."

The Apache nodded, then raised his eyebrows to question Kelly's next move.

"If you're wondering what I plan on doing, I intend to continue tracking him. I want to see where he goes and what he's up to. There's something about this whole thing that smells like skunk."

They rode down into the valley. Spotted Dog quickly picked up the trail of the four horses. Kelly planned to stay well back so whoever they were tracking wouldn't know they were there. He hoped that the man hadn't been aware of being trailed and therefore wouldn't be easily spooked, making a run for it and becoming much harder to find.

The desert was becoming more and more familiar to the marshal. Only a year before, he'd arrived in the nearby town of Desert Belle to investigate an explosion at the jail—an explosion that was reported to have killed the jail's occupants, the Bishop brothers. Kelly had been responsible for their incarceration after they had robbed a stagecoach of a military payroll. He, along with a squad of men from Fort Huachuca, had cornered the Bishop gang in a box canyon, captured them, and brought them to Desert Belle for trial. Kelly returned after the town's deputy sheriff hinted that he thought something was amiss concerning the explosion, even though there were two bodies in the rubble, presumably the bodies of the Bishops.

The episode brought back painful memories. He'd been shot and nearly killed himself. If he hadn't been found by a tough, indomitable woman driving a mule team, he'd probably have bled to death in the dirt. Then, Deputy Ben Satterfield, an old friend, was found murdered. If he never saw Desert Belle again, it would be too soon.

Spotted Dog pulled up, pointing off into the distance to where a road came down from the hills to the east. "It look like man meet white man's road over mountain."

"That road leads to Desert Belle. Maybe he's got business there. I reckon we'll find out soon enough. It's only about a four-hour ride from here."

"You want go in alone?"

"Nope. You're with me no matter what we

find. Besides, I may need you to back me up."

Spotted Dog grinned at the suggestion. As assurance that he'd be ready, he patted the Spencer rifle that he carried, a bandolier of .50-caliber cartridges draped across his chest.

"Let's camp here for the night. There's a small stream off about a quarter mile, if I'm remembering right. The man we're following might get spooked if we show up too soon after him, might figure out we were on his trail. U.S. Marshals likely don't show every day around here."

They rode to the creek, found a place to make camp, and dismounted. Kelly unsaddled the gelding while Spotted Dog went to round up some sticks for a fire. He took his rifle with him, so it came as no surprise when Kelly heard the roar of the Spencer echoing off the hills. He didn't even look up from building a fire pit when the Apache slipped silently into camp with a big grin on his face, some sticks under one arm, and a fat rabbit in his other hand.

"Well done, my friend. You build the fire, and I'll have that critter skinned and ready to cook in no time."

Spotted Dog nodded and set to his task.

The next morning, before they reached Desert Belle, Spotted Dog seemed reluctant to ride into the town. Kelly knew what was bothering him, and he spoke up before the Apache could register any reason for him to camp on the outskirts.

"What's bothering you, my friend?"

"Last time I go to white-eye's village, they put me in iron cage."

"That won't happen this time. Besides, I was there—nothing was going to happen. You remember, don't you?"

"Yes. Your word is true."

"Well, you got my word this time too. You're with me. I'll make sure nobody doubts that."

"Spotted Dog believe word of Kelly. I go."

Turning their mounts onto Galt Street brought back a flood of memories for Kelly, some good, some bad. The back part of the old adobe jail had been completely rebuilt, the façade refurbished. After Kelly put a stop to the crooked dealings of the manager of the Gilded Lily Mine, the town had seemed to come alive again. Several new businesses sprang up, and others expanded their operations. One sign that Desert Belle had a new confidence in its future was the general attitude of renewed hope and the promised infusion of new capital.

As they approached the outskirts, Kelly decided to make his first stop at the sheriff's office. Could this be the same Desert Belle he'd ridden away from only a year ago? Besides looking more prosperous, he noticed it seemed to have acquired numerous saloons, which meant gamblers and gun-slingers looking for easy pickings—or trouble.

Chapter Nine

Ten miles outside of Desert Belle, Quicksilver began acting strange, limping and lifting her right hind hoof as if she was trying to keep weight off it. Blue reined in and slid from the saddle. He went around and lifted the horse's leg to find the worst news possible: A shoe had split down the middle, and half of it was twisted and the nails were badly bent.

Damn, Quicksilver's come up lame. I got to do something. She can't travel no more like this. He began fishing around in his pants pocket until he came up with the folding knife his daddy had given him when he reached his fourteenth birthday. He swung out the blade and began prying at the broken shoe. *Maybe if I can get the darn thing off, it won't hurt her no more.*

That's when Quicksilver decided she'd had enough of Blue's digging at her hoof and gave him a little kick, dumping him in the dirt at the side of the road, then moving off several yards.

"Consarn it, you fool horse, can't you see I'm tryin' to help ya?" He wiped sweat off his brow and wished his hat hadn't left him several miles back. He was hot, tired, and in a near panic over this newest development hindering his quest to help Molly McQueen. He moved closer to the horse. Quicksilver took several more steps to avoid him. Blue was rapidly losing his temper.

"You fool horse! Why didn't I just take my white-faced mule? At least I wouldn't be left afoot in the blazin' sun!" he shouted. Quicksilver apparently didn't like his tone of voice; she moved off farther, just out of Blue's reach. The horse limped toward town, staying always a few feet ahead of Blue's ability to catch her. He gave up and began hoofing it along the road, trying to think what his next move should be now that it was clear he couldn't possibly make it to Desert Belle in time to get the letter onto the stagecoach.

Lost in pondering the various possibilities and wincing at the consequences of failure, he failed to notice that he had passed Quicksilver and was now leading this parade of two. The horse dutifully fell in behind, hobbling along, half dragging her hind leg. From off in the distance, Blue heard a heartening sound: the rumble of wagon wheels coming up behind him. He turned around to see a heavily laden wagon bearing down on him rapidly. He held up his hands to get the driver to stop. He watched as the driver hauled back on the reins of the four-horse team and slammed his foot against the brake handle. Blue stepped back off the road as the wagon came to a shuddering, dusty halt a few feet beyond where he had been standing.

"What's the problem, sonny? Need a ride—that it?"

"Uh, well, yessir, if you'd oblige. My horse threw a shoe and wouldn't let me pry it off so's we could get to town."

The driver wrapped the reins of his team around the brake handle and jumped down. Blue found he was looking up at the biggest man he'd ever seen, muscular and heavyset with hands as big as shovels. "Let's have a look at yer dilemma, sonny."

"I'd be grateful for your help, sir."

"Name's Bulger. I'm the blacksmith out at the Semper Mine. They needed someone to drive the ore wagon to Desert Belle, and I was the only hand available. So, here I am. What's your name?"

"Blue, sir. Blue LeBeau. I work at the Gilded Lily over thataway." Blue pointed off into the distance at where he thought the Lily was, although the road to town took so many turns, winding around and through boulder-strewn stretches, he really didn't have the slightest idea where the Lily was located. If the road was to get washed out, and all signs of it disappeared, he'd have one heck of a time finding his way home.

Bulger got Quicksilver's attention quickly, moving with the speed of a much smaller man.

Blue'd never seen such a big man move that fast before. The blacksmith grabbed the horse's reins and pulled her over to where Blue was standing, wide-eyed.

"Here, you take these reins, and don't you let go for anything. If this dern beast takes a notion to drag you into the next county, well, you just settle in for the ride. Understand?"

"Yessir. I'll hang on tight."

Bulger lifted the horse's hind leg, squinted at the damaged shoe, then, with one beefy, gloved hand took hold of the dangling iron end of the shoe and yanked it off as if it was no more than a toothpick he was snapping. He ran his glove over the rest of the shoe and frowned.

"Keep a hold on her while I get a pry bar off the wagon. I'll have the rest of that pesky shoe off right quick. Then you can be on your way."

"Thank you, sir."

Bulger pried the remaining piece of shoe off Quicksilver, patted the horse on the rump, and said, "That oughta get you to Desert Belle safe enough." He then climbed back up onto the high seat of the wagon, gave Blue a wink, and waved as he snapped the reins of his team.

Blue waved after him with a big grin. *Don't meet many folks today that'd help out a stranger on the road, especially a black boy.* He mounted Quicksilver before the horse could take a notion to reject being ridden any farther at all, having gotten used to just wandering behind her tormentor, broken shoe and all. They headed for Desert Belle at a trot.

When Blue and Quicksilver arrived in Desert Belle, he headed straight for the stage office after looping his horse's reins around a hitching rail. Quicksilver snorted a "don't be in any hurry to return" snort, which Blue ignored as he rushed up to the stage office door. He went inside and, seeing no one around, walked to the schedule posted on the wall. It stated in bold letters that the next stage to Tucson was at 4:30. The clock next to the schedule said the time was 5:20. Blue's hopes sank, and with them any possibility of saving Pooder's neck for losing the letter in the first place. He hung his head as he set out to find his friend, hoping that together they might find a way to save the day from being a total disaster. On his way out the door, he almost ran into the man he'd seen yelling orders to the stagecoach drivers and helping any pretty ladies off arrivals so they wouldn't get their skirts caught on the steps.

"Hold on there, boy. You lookin' for me?"

"Well, sorta, sir. I was tryin' to get this here letter on the stage for Tucson."

"You know how to read?"

"Uh, yessir."

"Then you already know that the stage left on time at four-thirty. My stagecoaches run on time, every time. Next one ain't for four days, same time. Come back then."

Blue thanked the man and excused himself, his mission a failure. His mood at that moment was as low as a snake's belly.

Outside, he looked up and down the main street, hoping to see Pooder's horse tied to one of the many rails along the wooden sidewalk. No such luck. He stopped in front of the town's only hotel in the shade of its overhanging balcony to think of the most likely place for Pooder to be— probably gambling away every last penny he had. And were it not for Blue's strong tendency to pinch every cent he made until it screamed in his pocket, Pooder would likely have lost all *his* money as well.

Blue decided to take a peek inside one of the three saloons that kept the town's main street abuzz with activity most any time of the day. He started with the Shot-to-Hell, only a couple doors down from the hotel. He looked over the swinging doors but saw neither hide nor hair of Zebulan Pooder. As a heavyset man appeared to be headed for the doors, wobbling and bumping into chairs and tables as he came, Blue stepped back to keep from being bowled over. Outside, the man stopped to shade his eyes from the sun, obviously a shock after the dimness of the cave-like saloon. He let out a belch, then grabbed for a post to keep from toppling over.

Blue spoke up as the man steadied himself. "Sir, would you know if Zebulan Pooder was here recently?"

The man turned, bleary-eyed, and muttered something about Pooder's having been chased out earlier by the three Clutter brothers for leaving the game before he was flat broke. Then the man let out a roar of laughter, after which he stumbled out into the street, trying to negotiate his way to the other side without being run down by two riders who were at that moment passing by.

Run out by three brothers? That's not good news. Where would he go? I'd better check with the sheriff. Maybe something's happened to him. Blue was suddenly awash with concern.

Blue trotted down Galt Street to where it turned and started uphill toward Mrs. Dunham's boarding house. Just before the bend in the road sat the adobe jail and sheriff's office. Blue stepped inside with a shudder. Instantly, he was struck by the remembrance of his last visit to this building. It had been under less than desirable circumstances. A year back, he and Pooder had arrived there, being chased by the notorious Bishop brothers and a couple of other gun-slingers, after Pooder had unwittingly shot down one of their gang. In fact, the two boys had racked up a total of three dead outlaws by the time they got to Desert Belle, and the sheriff wasn't taking kindly to their presence.

Blue opened the door to find a new sheriff, a man who looked like he meant business when it came to handling a gun. Tall, gaunt, and well dressed, Sheriff Hawk Burns looked up as the nervous boy approached his desk.

Burns leaned back. "Now, just what is it you want here, boy?"

"Uh, sir, er, Sheriff, I was wonderin' if you might have seen a friend of mine, another boy 'bout my age named Zebulan Pooder."

"Do I look like a man who gives a hoot about your friend, unless of course he's done broke the law? Has he? Is that why you're here?" Sheriff Burns stood up, squinting at Blue as if the boy had the word *criminal* painted on his forehead.

"Why, no, sir. He's an honest soul, no doubt about that. But, you see, he's, uh, missin', and I been sent to find him. So, I figured if there was anyone in town who'd know just about everything that goes on, well, that'd be the sheriff."

"Uh-huh. Butterin' me up ain't goin' to find your friend. And anyway, I ain't seen no boys around here. So, go on with you, and stop botherin' a busy lawman. Now, git." The sheriff turned back to his desk. Blue wasted no time following the sheriff's instructions to light a shuck out of there or face the consequences.

As Blue made his way back to where he'd tied Quicksilver, he overheard some men laughing and slapping their thighs at something that must have been powerful funny. When he got close enough to make out what they were laughing about, he heard one of them mention Pooder's name.

"Lawsy, did you see that boy shake the dust off'n his boots with the Clutters not ten steps behind him? Why, they'll skin him alive if they find he was holdin' out on 'em." Everyone laughed.

Blue moved closer. He sidled up to one of the men and asked, "Sir, did you happen to see which direction ol' Pooder went?"

The man looked down at Blue and grinned a toothless grin. "I don't rightly know for sure, but it looked to me like he was headed back to the Gilded Lily. It's likely he was goin' back so's he could conjure up some more cash to lose to them Clutters." The man snickered at the thought.

"Would you happen to know how long ago that was?"

"Why? He owe you money too?"

"Oh, no, sir. I, uh—"

"If you was figurin' to save him from his foolish ways, well, I reckon you're a mite late, 'cause the Cluttters got first dibs on 'im." The crowd broke out into uproarious laughter once again.

Blue walked away from the men, dejected and down. He'd been expected to save the day by getting that important letter to the stagecoach office before it left for Tucson. Pooder had failed Molly, and now he had too. He shook his head in self-recrimination. Then, out of the corner of his eye, he saw movement from the side of the building near where he stood. He looked into the shadows, and there, huddled close to the ground, half-hidden by some crates, was Pooder in the flesh. He ran to where his friend was hiding.

"Hey, Pooder—"

"Shh, you fool! You want to get me killed?"

Chapter Ten

Blue was startled by Pooder's words. He moved back into the shadows near where his friend was holed up, hoping to learn what was going on. When he was only a couple of feet away, Pooder shot out a hand, grabbed Blue by the shirt, and pulled him down. They were now both hunkered down behind empty crates left over from several shipments to the general store. The two were reduced to whispering to each other to avoid detection. Blue, of course, had no idea why the need for such secrecy or whom they were hiding from. Pooder yanked harder on Blue's shirt, pulling him even closer.

"You can't tell anyone you saw me, you understand?" Pooder's eyes were full of fear, mixed with a healthy amount of confusion.

"Uh, yeah, sure, but what's going on? Did you shoot someone again?"

"No, I didn't shoot no one. But I got a little problem. Some nasty gents are after me, and if they find me, they'll likely feed me to the hogs. So promise you won't sell me out."

"Of course I wouldn't let on I saw you. Why would I?"

Pooder released his grip and looked down ashamedly.

"So what'd you do this time?" Blue knew that look on Pooder's face. He'd been through Pooder's trials and tribulations enough to last a lifetime. He was wearying of trying to cover up for his friend's shortcomings.

"I didn't do anything. I was having a bad day at the poker table, that's all. When I tried to quit, the Clutter brothers wouldn't let me. So I ran. They're out there somewhere looking to skin me alive so they can take every last dime. I held out on 'em a mite. I always keep a few extra greenbacks tucked down in my boot. Maybe they found out about that. Hey, you know that. Say, you didn't tell nobody, did you?"

"Of course I didn't tell nobody. What do you take me for? Besides, that ain't the worst of your troubles. You dropped Molly's letter and didn't get it to the stage before it left for Tucson. Molly's pretty mad. I'm not sure you still got a job. And without regular pay, how the hell are you going to spend every free minute gambling? Huh? Answer that."

"Yeah, uh, the letter. Reckon I did mess that up pretty good, didn't I? I remembered the letter just before the Clutters started givin' chase. I knew I'd lost it somewhere. What am I goin' to do now?"

"Well, I brought it to town to try to get it on the stage, but that blasted Quicksilver threw a shoe.

93

Then she tried to run away from me. If it hadn't been for a wagon that came by from another mine, I'd still be out there on that road, hoofin' it. As it was, I missed the stage. Now I got to figure what to do, myself. Molly said it had to get to this fellow, pronto. Can't even send a telegram, 'cause it has to be delivered in person."

Blue pulled the folded and wrinkled letter from his shirt pocket. It was dirty, and a corner was torn. He stared at it as if it were a rattlesnake about to strike. He sighed and stuffed it back into his pocket. "I figure we both got big problems."

Pooder's formerly frightened expression suddenly turned thoughtful. He scrunched up his face and began chewing his lower lip. "Hmm," he muttered.

Blue caught the change in Pooder's demeanor and reacted quickly. "Oh, no, you don't, Pooder."

"What?" Pooder's eyes got wide, and his expression turned to that of someone unjustly accused of a crime. "I didn't say anything."

"You don't have to. I know that look. Every time it comes over you, I find myself in big trouble. And I ain't up for no trouble—at least no more'n I already got, thanks to you."

"Well, okay, if that's the way you feel about it. I just won't toss in my two cents' worth and maybe save the day. You can go on about your way, and I'll make out. Somehow."

Blue saw through Pooder's bluff, but he was

hesitant to forego the chance that his friend's overactive imagination might someday come up with a good idea, not that it was likely. But miracles did happen, and his momma always told him to be open to such possibilities. He sighed and looked away before speaking.

"Okay. I'll listen just this one more time. But if it even *smells* like somethin' a cow leaves behind, I'm on my way. And you're on your own. Under-stand?"

"Uh-huh," muttered Pooder, but he really wasn't listening. He was busy putting the finishing touches on his latest scheme.

"One more thing. Before I go anywhere, I got to get Quicksilver shoed proper. Why don't I go on down to the blacksmith and see about that, while you're cogitatin', of course?" Blue started to get up, then noticed that Pooder hadn't heard a word he'd said. "Uh, Pooder, did you hear me?"

"Uh-huh, sure. I've almost got my fine idea ready. You gotta be patient."

"As usual, you aren't listenin'. I said I'm goin' to the smithy to get Quicksilver's shoe fixed. I'll be back soon. You just stay here." This time, Blue didn't hesitate. He got up and marched back down the street where he'd tied the troublesome mare.

He was shaking his head as he was nearly knocked off the boardwalk by three rough-looking characters. They seemed to be looking for some-thing . . . or someone. A chill ran up Blue's back.

Could these hombres be the Clutter brothers that Pooder was so scared of? One of them grumbled about how folks should know their place and not get in the way of men with important business. Blue scooted off to gather up his horse, looking over his shoulder to see if the three men entered the alley where Pooder was hiding. Fortunately, they walked on by, so Blue figured his friend was safe. For the moment, at least.

Blue walked Quicksilver to the blacksmith's. It was located at the side of the livery. When he handed over the horse's reins, the smithy told him to come back in two, three hours. Blue started to protest that he couldn't wait that long but thought better of it and walked away, figuring to put together a plan of his own. Waiting on Pooder to come up with an idea with any merit at all would likely end up with them both in more hot water than they already were in.

When he returned to the spot where he'd left Pooder, he was shocked to see the alley empty. *Great! Where can that fool have gone off to now?* He looked all around. There was no sign of him. Since he hadn't seen Pooder's horse when he rode into town, he figured Pooder had left her at the livery so she wouldn't have to stand at the hitching rail all the time he was inside playing cards. And losing all his money, of course.

Blue ran down the board walkway, dodging people coming out of stores and old men sitting on benches outside the saloons. He nearly knocked over a woman with an armful of packages who stepped out the door of the general store while talking back over her shoulder. Blue managed a sorry excuse for an apology, which was returned with a curt, "Well, I never," from the aloof woman, who simply stuck her nose farther into the air and stormed off.

He was nearly out of breath by the time he reached the wide-open doors to the livery. Henry Banister, the liveryman, was sweeping straw out of the doorway and into a stall.

"Mr. Banister, have you seen Zeb Pooder recent like?"

"Uh, well, I seem to recall him, uh, comin' around yesterday, or was it the day before? Hmmm."

Just then, Pooder stepped out from behind some bags of feed with a sheepish grin. "It's okay, Mr. Banister. Blue here is a friend. I didn't mean him when I asked you not to let on you'd seen me. But I thank you just the same." He took Blue by the arm and led him back into the narrow, dark confines of the old barn.

"Where'd you go? I thought you was going to stay put," Blue said with a touch of bitterness in his voice.

A big horsefly drifted by Blue's face, from which he involuntarily ducked back. He took a wide swipe at the critter, missing it by a mile. The fly zigzagged slowly toward the stalls at the rear, where he was sure to find a meal. A horse whinnied from somewhere just outside.

"The Clutters came by, nosin' around. I couldn't take the chance they wouldn't come down the alley. Sorry. How'd you know to come lookin' here?"

"I figured you'd at least have the good sense to put your horse up, since you planned on makin' another long day of it at the gambling tables. Didn't take a genius to figure that out. Even *you* wouldn't want your horse to stand in the sun all day without water."

"Okay, okay. I said I'm sorry."

"Never mind. Now, what's this great plan you got all worked out? We got to do something, and quick."

As Pooder began to elaborate, he heard Mr. Banister talking unusually loudly.

"Why, hello, boys. You Clutters lookin' to retrieve your horses? Or will you be stayin' another day?"

"Yeah, we're leavin' right away, so go ahead and bring out our mounts and get 'em saddled. Reckon we're goin' for a little ride," Hank Clutter said.

"I'll fetch 'em straightaway. You boys can make yourselves comfortable there under that tree if you've a mind to. Have a drink of cold water from the well. If you've got a long ride ahead of you, might want to fill your canteens too."

"We ain't goin' that far, just out to the Lily, old man." Joe Clutter spoke up.

Hank slapped his brother on the shoulder. "Hush your mouth, little brother, and don't go tellin' the whole world our business."

Shamefacedly, Joe hung his head and muttered, "Sorry."

When Banister came to the rear of the livery barn to fetch the Clutters' horses, he saw that his loud talk had given the boys sufficient warning to get themselves hidden behind a workbench set up to repair harnesses. He winked as he walked by, whistling.

"Whew, that was close," whispered Blue. "Those Clutters seem to be everywhere."

"That's for sure. And I'll tell you, they're the meanest three owlhoots I ever laid eyes on. Worst thing I ever done, lettin' them get their hooks into me. But I've learned my lesson—don't you think I ain't. No, sir. From now on, I'm playin' nothing but sure things, like faro."

Blue shook his head in disbelief at what he was hearing.

After the Clutter brothers had ridden away, Blue and Pooder crawled out of their hiding place and dusted themselves off. The dust made Blue sneeze and cough. Pooder rolled his eyes at him like he was a momma's boy. They walked to the front of the livery, where Mr. Banister was getting ready to continue his sweeping.

"Thanks, Mr. Banister, for not givin' us up to them three," Pooder said. "They sure are an ornery lot."

"More'n ornery, son, they're pure evil. When they get their hooks into a man, why, he's a goner. I've heard tell of folks that never come back after a night of cards with those three."

"You mean, they'd kill a body?" Pooder said, his eyes the size of poached eggs.

"That's exactly what I mean. Trouble is, that sheriff don't seem to have the gumption to do a darn thing about it. Reckon the citizens will just have to keep a keen eye out and avoid any invitation to take a chance on gettin' rich, which they ain't." Banister took a couple of swipes at the floor with his beat-up old broom; then he stopped and got a thoughtful look on his face. "Come to think of it, Hank Clutter did ask if I'd seen you fellas."

"Uh-oh. Wh-What'd you tell 'im?"

"Told 'im I didn't recall seein' you for several days. Joe looked suspicious, but Hank said you could wait. Said they had other fish to fry. And off they rode. Got the feelin' they'll be back real soon, though."

The boys said good-bye to Banister and retrieved their horses. As they mounted up, Blue turned to Pooder and said, "I'm still waitin' to hear about your great plan to get this letter to Tucson. If we don't come up with somethin' quick like, Molly's gonna be real mad."

Pooder got a sick look on his face.

Chapter Eleven

Marshal Kelly and Spotted Dog rode into Desert Belle midmorning. The town was already bustling with activity. A slow-moving, high-sided wagon rumbled down the middle of the street, forcing riders and pedestrians alike to step aside or be crushed beneath its ponderous, creaking wheels. The town brought back memories for Kelly, many of which he would have just as soon forgotten. Spotted Dog watched the lines form around the marshal's mouth and the reflection of bad times darken his face.

"This place have bad spirits?"

"Some. When I was here last, a friend was murdered, and some very evil men escaped and nearly stole a gold shipment. A lot of folks died."

"Maybe better this time."

"I hope so. We'll stop at the sheriff's office to see if he's noticed any strangers riding into town the last few hours. Maybe someone caught sight of the man we been trailin'."

With Kelly leading the way, the two rode slowly through the center of town, past the many new establishments that hadn't been there when the marshal was last in Desert Belle. There were now three saloons and a dress shop, a shoe store, and some new competition for the general store. There was a place where a fellow could buy nothing but hats, and another that specialized in shoes and boots of every type and style. The town had even acquired a brothel, although Kelly saw that as a step backward. The hotel had been spiffed up with a coat of paint, and new draperies adorned the windows. When they got to where Galt Street turned uphill, Kelly was warmed by the sight of Mrs. Dunham's boarding house still standing sentry at the end of the block, freshly painted and now adorned with new green shutters to keep the dust out whenever a storm was about to come a-blowing.

They reined in at the hitching rail in front of the wooden sign dangling from a pole that stuck out from the adobe building. The sign said, SHERIFF HAWK BURNS.

As they started to dismount, a man with a badge emerged from the door to the jail. He was tall and lean, wore narrow suspenders over a white cotton shirt, and sported a slouch hat that was frayed around the brim. He held a coach gun in his right hand, aimed at Kelly. His face wore the scars of too many confrontations, too much whiskey, and not an ounce of joy to keep him sane. And he looked as if he meant business.

"Mister, I don't know who you are, but if you know what's good for you, you'll take my advice and get that damned Injun out of my town, pronto. And I'd do it before this well-armed officer of the law loses what little patience he's got left."

Kelly slowly stepped down off his black gelding, pulled his Winchester carbine from its scabbard, and took a couple of easy steps toward the sheriff. He pulled his vest back enough to reveal the U.S. Marshal badge.

"We got business here, Sheriff, and we're goin' nowhere until it's finished. So, what say we all get inside out of this blisterin' sun and talk things over?" Kelly motioned for Spotted Dog to dismount and follow as he started for the door. The sheriff hesitated for a moment, a brief look of indecision on his face, then stepped aside with a wave of his hand.

"Sorry I took you for a scoundrel, Marshal. Been nothin' but riffraff driftin' into town ever since another mine hit a fair to middlin' vein, not ten miles to the west. Sit and have a coffee with me."

Kelly nodded his acceptance and chose to sit in a rickety straight-back chair with its back to the inner wall, so he could watch both the sheriff and the door. He had no particular reason to assume this sheriff was anything other than what he pretended to be: a small-town officer of the law, just trying to do his duty. But Kelly's experience of late with lawmen who'd overstepped their boundaries tended to make him more suspicious than most.

"Don't suppose your heathen friend here would like a cup. I hear Injuns don't generally take to partakin' in the white man's evil brew." Burns cast a snide grin at the Apache, almost as if he assumed Spotted Dog spoke no English.

"Spotted Dog, here, happens to like coffee almost as much as I dislike folks that figure he ain't civilized. He'll accept a cup, thank you," Kelly said, bitterness in his voice as he was reminded of the treatment his friend had received at the hands of Sheriff John Henry Stevens' murdering and thieving deputy. He held a steady, discomforting gaze on the sheriff.

Taking notice of the marshal's seeming belligerence at anything that might smack of disapproval of the Indian, Burns reluctantly poured three cups, handing one to each man. He took off his hat and sat back in his rickety swiveling desk chair.

"And now, sir, to what do I owe this visit to our community?"

Kelly's lip curled, as he knew so much more than this sheriff was apparently aware of as it pertained to Desert Belle's history.

"We been trackin' three, maybe four men for quite a spell. It appears, or at least Spotted Dog seems inclined to think, that three of the men were dead before they left Cochise. The fourth man may have dynamited a narrow canyon to serve as a tomb of sorts for the other three and maybe throw us off his trail. I'm figuring that lone rider may have come to town recently, in the last day or so. He'd likely have been leadin' three other horses."

Burns leaned back. He scratched at his stubbly chin as his eyes sought an answer in the ceiling.

"Don't recollect any faces I ain't seen before, but that don't mean he ain't here. I can't check on every soul that comes to town. And I don't have any deputies, though heaven knows I could use a couple. I'll ask around, see if any of the bartenders have run across any strangers. That suit you?"

Kelly and Spotted Dog emptied their cups at almost the same time, stood, and handed the empties back to the sheriff. "Suits me fine. Much obliged. We'll be in town for a couple days. You run across anything you think might be interestin', you just holler." Kelly touched the brim of his cavalry-style Stetson and followed the Apache outside.

As he slipped his carbine back into the saddle scabbard, he whispered to Spotted Dog, "That fella is either holdin' out on us, or he spends too much time hidin' behind his desk."

"You think he know more than he tell?"

"Indeed, I do. And I intend to find out what that is." Kelly swung into his saddle.

"Where we go now?" Spotted Dog said as he mounted up.

"If I was leadin' three extra horses across the desert and I came to a town that seemed like it was up and coming, the first thing I'd do is try to sell those extra mounts. I think we'll amble on down and check the livery, first thing."

Memories surrounded Kelly as he guided his gelding down the main street, images of what had been a dying community when last he was here. He could almost see Deputy Ben Satterfield standing next to him, laughing and raising a toast to the capture of the Bishop brothers. He stared wistfully at the bat-wing doors of the Shot-to-Hell Saloon. That was the last place he'd seen the amiable deputy alive.

He turned the gelding sharply and reined up in front of the saloon. "You stay with the horses, Spotted Dog, while I visit an old source of information."

The Apache took the reins of Kelly's mount as the marshal stomped up the steps and disappeared through the double doors. Smoke drifted out as the bat-wings swung to a stop on their hinges. From inside, the Indian could hear laughter, the sound of voices raised in drunken bliss. He just shook his head in wonderment at what little it took to entertain the white man.

Kelly looked around the room, then spotted the bartender returning to his post after delivering beer to a table of boisterous cowboys. He recognized the man behind the new oak bar as the same bartender who'd been in charge the day he came looking for answers about the bodies found in the rubble of the jail the day of that fateful explosion. The bartender recognized him too.

"Howdy, Marshal. Ain't seen you for quite a spell. What can I get you to drink?"

"Same as last time—nothing. I'm lookin' for information again. Have you seen a stranger come through those doors in the past twenty-four hours, alone and dusty?"

The bartender picked up a wet towel and began wiping the bar in front of Kelly as he scrunched up his mouth in thought.

"There was a fella come in here this mornin', but he only stayed long enough for one beer. Then he slipped out while I was cleanin' up some of them tables in the back."

"What'd he look like?"

"Looked like he could afford more'n one beer."

"Can you describe him?"

"Now that you mention it, I don't remember anything that might set him off from a hundred other fellas that come in here regular. I reckon you could say he was 'average' in a way, but wearin' better'n average clothes. Had on a pair of them stovepipe boots, like the ones you're a-wearin', and a leather vest with silver buttons. Don't recall if he had a mustache or not. Don't think so. Dark felt hat."

Kelly tossed down two bits for the beer he hadn't had and said thanks. The bartender scooped up the coin and dropped it into his pocket. It amounted to a tip for what little information he knew. "Should I try lookin' you up if he drops in again?" he called after the retreating lawman.

Kelly nodded a yes as he slipped through the doors and out into the bright sun. Spotted Dog was seated on the edge of the porch where the overhang afforded some shade. He had led the horses to a watering trough and tied them close by so they could drink whenever they were of a mind.

Kelly and the Apache walked their horses the block down to the livery. A man wielding a pitchfork met them at the door. His well-lined face broke into a cheery smile as he saw what looked like business approaching.

"Afternoon, gents. Lookin' for a place to bed them critters for the night?"

"No, but I could do with a little information, if you could oblige," Kelly said, making certain the liveryman took notice of his badge.

"What is it you want to know?"

"Have you met up with a man new to town in the last twenty-four hours, leading three horses? Bartender said he was wearin' boots like mine."

"Yep. Right nice gent he was too. Polite and reasonable."

"Reasonable?"

"Yep. Took my first offer with nary a quibble, not that it wasn't fair."

"Took your first offer?"

"Why, yeah, my offer to buy them three cayuses off of him. I didn't figure he had need of all three. He didn't have the look of a drover."

"You bought his horses?"

"Yep, or at least three of 'em. Fine animals they are too. Want to look?"

"I think that would be a good idea. Did he sell you the saddles also?"

"Matter of fact, he threw them in for the price of the horses. They'll clean up real good."

"That wouldn't happen to be the saddles hangin' over that rail, would it?"

"Right you are, Marshal. All three of 'em."

Kelly walked over to the saddles and leaned in to get a better look at some stains. "This looks like blood to me. What's it look like to you?"

The liveryman leaned over and squinted, then stood up straight. "I reckon it could be; can't rightly say."

"Might be a good idea to inform the sheriff. If these are the horses we been followin', they likely don't belong to the man you bought them from."

"Stolen? Damn! I been hornswaggled. I reckon

I'll lose the money too." The liveryman scratched at his balding head as he bit his lower lip.

"I doubt the men who owned these horses will be makin' a claim anytime soon. Unless they can claw their way out from under half a mountainside."

Chapter Twelve

Abner Dillard was busy at his ledger when Molly came into his office. He looked around to catch a glimpse of her ambling over to his unmade cot. The stretched canvas made a sound akin to tearing cloth as she dropped onto it. Molly was not a small woman, but Abner was comforted by the knowledge that no damage could be done, since the cot had been designed by the Army to accommodate the weight of much heavier men. Abner had picked it up from a sutler's store at Fort Huachuca several years before. He kept the cot in his office and insisted on sleeping there. He said he liked the idea of being able to rest whenever he wanted. It also came in handy when he traveled. And he seemed to be traveling often. At least that's the impression he'd given when he lapsed into a lengthy treatise on his vast experience as a bookkeeper when he applied for the job at the Gilded Lily.

"Numbers are the only friends I need," he'd repeated on several occasions when asked why he hadn't taken advantage of the more comfortable accommodations in the bunkhouse, where a man might find a friendly game of poker or hear a good joke.

Dillard claimed not sleeping in his own bed made him uncomfortable, as well as desiring to never be far from his work. According to Abner, his work *was* his life, the only family he had, and he had made it his priority. All of which made Molly a little suspicious of him, but her desperate need for a bookkeeper outweighed her misgivings.

But then, Abner wasn't the sociable type, preferring instead to live hermitlike, keeping close company with the one person who didn't constantly arouse his qualms about one thing or another: himself. Right then, he was wondering why the mine manager had settled on that particular time for a visit. After all, he was clearly engrossed in something more important than chitchat, a distraction for which he let it be known he had neither time nor patience.

"Uh, is there something I can do for you, ma'am?" He dipped his pen into the glass inkwell and went back to scratching another entry on the page of his great book.

"I just wondered when Mr. Bond indicated he'd have the money at the Desert Belle Bank. Has he been in touch?"

"I received a telegram just a week ago that he would accompany the money to the bank a day or two after receiving our letter of intent. He said he would leave Tucson immediately thereafter."

"A letter he won't receive for a couple more days, I'd guess, since Pooder temporarily lost it." Molly balled her fists as she muttered something about throttling Pooder when next she saw him. "I am sorta curious, though, as to why Mr. Bond wanted the letter addressed to a post office box instead of to him personally."

"Yes, ma'am, that is a curiosity. However, I figure he knows best how to conduct his business. While we're talkin' on it, how about if I were to travel to town and stay at the hotel for a few days, just in case he arrives before we expect him? We can't afford to miss him; wouldn't you agree?"

"Yes, I s'pose that would be the smart thing to do. That way *you* can see to the transfer of his money to our account, making certain he has lived up to his side of the bargain," Molly said with a sigh of resignation. She chewed on her lip as she continued to puzzle over how the mine could have gotten into such a sad financial condition without her being aware of it.

"I'll prepare to leave with the wagon when it goes in for the new block-and-tackle assemblies. The boys have been struggling to keep some of the old ones from coming apart with heavy loads. An injury could occur almost anytime without repairs."

"Tell the hotel clerk to bill us for your room. Come back as soon as you have the transaction complete. I reckon our new partner will want to come out and inspect the place too."

"I assume that is a possibility, although he has not expressed such a desire," Abner said, closing the ledger and placing his pen in a tray made out of a piece of petrified wood from the North Country.

Molly pushed herself up off of the cot and walked across the room but stopped at the open door. Her eyes narrowed as she turned back to Abner with a frown. "You know, I been wonderin' why this Mr. Bond didn't want to see the operation *before* agreein' to the deal."

"I have been led to understand he's a businessman who has been involved in mining for several years. I doubt he has any need to see a mine that's likely no different from hundreds of others. I also am led to believe that this isn't the first mine he's invested in."

"Hmm," Molly grunted, closing the door behind her. As the latch bolt clicked into place, it was like a knife in her back. Her conversation with Abner Dillard hadn't eased her discomfort with the whole situation, her puzzlement over how the mine operation could have taken such a precipitous downturn right when she had been feeling strongly that all was in order. She had been happy, the bank was happy she'd been able to pay off their note, and the miners seemed happy with their wages and reasonable working conditions. What could possibly have happened? She was in need of closure on the whole matter. But numbers didn't lie. And Abner's numbers spelled out a clear, unmistakable tale of failure. At least, that's how it appeared.

She walked slowly back across the barren yard to the shack where the mine foreman had an office of sorts. He was seldom there, but on the off chance he might be in, she figured finding someone to talk to might help keep her mind off her misery. As she pulled on the creaky door, she thought she heard a sound coming from around back. She let the door swing closed again and followed a well-worn path around the small building, coming face-to-face with the foreman just as he was lifting a whiskey bottle to his lips. When he saw her, he dropped the bottle into the dirt. It shattered on impact, splattering the brown liquid onto his boots and denims and staining the ground a rust color.

"Uh, sorry, Miss Molly. I didn't hear you comin'." The foreman's face turned a disturbing red, almost as if he were experiencing a heart attack. Perspiration popped out on his broad forehead like dew on the morning grass.

"I can see that, Mr. Mowbry. Sorry about your bottle. I might have been enticed to share a drink or two with you if you'd managed to keep a tighter grip."

"I, uh, don't d-do this kind of thing often, you

understand. It's just that I been hearin' a rumor goin' around that you intend to sell the Lily, and the boys an' me, well, we ain't certain we'll still have our jobs, if that were to happen."

She sighed and chewed her lower lip. "I have never lied to you, Mr. Mowbry, and I'll not start now. What you've been hearing is partly true. I've agreed to take on a partner in order to keep the mine going. You see, the bookkeeper has shown me that we are losing an alarming amount of money. If we continue on this path, we'll have to shut 'er down. It's sad but true."

"How on earth can that be, ma'am? We been takin' ore outta here somethin' ferocious. Good grade too. You certain he knows what he's talkin' about?"

"I been wonderin' the same, but figures don't lie."

"Hmm. I got no use for folks who spend their whole lives jottin' down ciphers in little columns. I say let 'em go below and see for themselves what minin's all about. I doubt old Abner has a lick of sense when it comes to puttin' pick to rock."

Molly thought about that for a moment. She caught herself thinking along the same lines as the foreman, but it wasn't something she'd ever let on about. She had great respect for folks who could keep records with such precision, keeping the lines in perfect order. A soul who had been trained in ciphering was a person of wonder to her, and the ability to keep in one's head all those jots and tittles was certainly a marvel. She just naturally trusted a person like that implicitly. And for that reason, she never questioned Abner Dillard's word. She heaved a great sigh and turned to walk away from the foreman.

"Tell the boys not to worry none about their jobs. I ain't expectin' to be making changes," she called back over her shoulder.

But as she wandered to her own office, that very thought became a puzzlement to her. If the new partner expected to keep everything just as it was, why wouldn't he expect to continue losing money? Why would any good business-man purposely invest in a money-losing proposi-tion? The frown on her face took on all the characteristics of an impending thunderstorm, dark and foreboding. Her pace quickened. When she got to the building where her office sat below that of Abner Dillard's, she knocked on his door. There was no answer. She turned the knob and peeked inside. The room was empty. She went to the corral to see if the wagon was ready to leave for town.

"Bob, have you seen Abner?"

"Yes, ma'am. He left with the parts wagon goin' into Desert Belle. Left about ten minutes ago. Looked like he was fixin' to stay awhile too. Had two suitcases with him."

• • •

The wagon dropped Abner off in front of the hotel. He lifted his two cases down from the high seat and struggled up the steps under their weight. Inside, he pinged the bell for the desk clerk, who greeted him as he came from a back room.

"Afternoon, Mr. Dillard. What can I do for you?"

"I'll be needing a room for a couple days. Charge it to the Lily. It's business."

"Yes, sir. If you'll sign the register, please, I'll get your key."

Abner carried the cases up to his room and quickly slid them under the bed. He parted the lace curtains to look down onto the street. Several horses were tied to the hitching rails in front of the three saloons. He smiled as he considered joining in a game of chance, a rarely indulged interest. But, under his present circumstances, perhaps not such a bad idea. He looked into the slightly askew Chatham mirror, licked his fingers to smooth down a few wild hairs, and left his room, being careful to lock the door behind him.

He must have had the look of a sucker on his face, because he had no more than entered the Shot-to-Hell Saloon than he saw the Clutter brothers come through the bat-wing doors and settle at a table. Seeing Abner, they invited him to join in a game of poker. He accepted. He quickly found out that winning at poker wasn't as easy as it looked. After an hour, he was down nearly a hundred dollars. That much money was, to a bookkeeper, an enormous amount to lose in a game of chance. His confidence waning, Abner Dillard decided it was time to bow out and return to his room for the night. The Clutters weren't pleased at his verbal attempts to make a hasty exit.

A tall stranger wearing black stovepipe boots stood at the bar with an amused smile on his lips. He turned to the bartender and asked, "Who's the scrawny fool that got himself sucked in by those tinhorns?"

The bartender looked over at the Clutters' gathering and responded, "That's the bookkeeper out at the Gilded Lily. Name's Abner Dillard, I believe. Comes in once in a while for a shot or two. Never saw him get caught up gambling before, though."

"He don't appear to be doin' too well. Someone ought to rescue the little twerp before he loses his whole bankroll."

"Probably, but it ain't gonna be me, mister. Those Clutter boys don't take kindly to folks interferin' with their game," the bartender said, slowly moving down the bar.

The stranger strolled over to the game, looked on for a moment, then said, "Abner, the boss needs you right away. Sent me to get you."

Abner looked around with a puzzled expression. "Uh, I don't—"

The stranger pulled Abner out of his chair, scooped up what funds he still had lying on the table, dropping them into Abner's hat, and started him for the door. "Sorry, gents, business comes first."

Dillard was clearly confused by the stranger's actions but relieved to be out of a game he couldn't win. He muttered a weak "thanks" to the man gripping his arm tightly.

As they pushed through the swinging doors, Abner looked at the man and said, "Thanks, stranger. Say, where we headed?"

"Someplace where we can talk, private like."

Chapter Thirteen

After Kelly had examined all three horses and the saddles and saddlebags of the presumably dead men, he took special notice of splotches of what appeared to be dried blood on the cantle, seat, and fender of each one. *Sure as shootin', someone badly wounded, or worse, was occupyin' these saddles, and recently.* He was now firmly convinced that Spotted Dog's intuition was a thing to accept without further question. After a cordial acknowledgment of the liveryman's help, he and Spotted Dog rode out of town a mile or so to make camp.

A dribbling creek wandered down from one of the nearby peaks and through an arroyo with plenty of grass and a few ash and willow trees. They followed the creek to a spot where the trees offered a good spot to build a fire and settle in for the night. The spot also afforded a clear view of the main road to Desert Belle without revealing their own location. Kelly unsaddled the black gelding and tossed his saddle blanket on the ground. He then hobbled the horse and set him free to graze and drink wherever he wished.

Spotted Dog knew instinctively what his job

was expected to be. He took his Spencer and, following the creek toward the foothills, sprinted off into the brush. Kelly smiled to himself at how perceptive the Apache was. He also knew that it would be only a short time before he heard the roar of the big-bore rifle, followed by the quick return of the Chiricahua with dinner. He built a fire and scooped up clean water from the fast-running creek. They'd have coffee and beans in minutes.

Kelly pulled his field glasses from the saddle-bag and scanned the road below. He saw no human movement along the road. Then his attention was diverted as an echoing boom came as expected, and Spotted Dog didn't disappoint when, without a sound, he seemed to appear out of nowhere with a rabbit dangling from his belt. *I'm sure glad he's on my side.*

"That didn't take long," Kelly said.

"Smell coffee. I hurry." The Apache had a wide grin on his weathered face. He tossed the rabbit to the ground in front of the marshal, who set to skinning the critter with a deft hand and a very sharp knife.

Spotted Dog squatted near the fire as the cooling shadows of dusk crept over them. The sky was clear and promised a full moon. After eating, Kelly began rambling aloud to reconstruct the events that had brought them to this place, even though he assumed Spotted Dog would find the whole thing more amusing than informative.

"Since that fella the liveryman was tellin' us about was last seen taking this road, I have to assume he'll come back this way sooner or later, since it goes right by the Gilded Lily Mine."

"He have business there?"

"That's a good question. But since we don't actually know who the surviving member of the original four is, there's no way to make a connection with the mining operation. If it is this Alex Bond, who is supposedly some sort of businessman, maybe he's interested in investing. But if the man is one of the bounty hunters, what could he possibly find of interest at a mine?"

Kelly removed his Stetson and scratched his head, then finger-combed his long hair back into place. "I'm not even sure what it is *I'm* doin' out here. I can't even prove there's been a crime."

"Three dead men," the Apache mumbled.

"*Maybe* three dead men. I don't have even one body."

"Three horses with blood on saddles," the Indian reminded him.

"They coulda cut themselves on some barbwire or rode through a forest of cholla. A little blood ain't proof positive of a crime. I need somethin' more—"

"Like man who sell horses?"

"Yep. Just like that."

"Want me to scout mine? See if he go there?"

123

At Spotted Dog's suggestion, Kelly's previously relaxed mind kicked into gear and began to conjure up possibilities. *Maybe it would be a good idea to send Spotted Dog out to do what he does best: scouting. It sure won't hurt none to know for sure whether that fella reached the Lily or not.*

"Good idea. No sense goin' at night, but at first light, maybe you could scout out whether our friend did ride out this way, while I stand guard here to make sure he don't slip by us."

The Apache nodded with a satisfied grin. The white marshal had approved of his idea, a confirmation of his worthiness. A bond of trust was beginning to grow stronger between them. Trust was in short supply on the reservation, where almost every white man who had contact with the Indians at San Carlos was suspicious and fearful of meaningful interaction. Marshal Kelly seemed to be the exception, rather than the rule, and Spotted Dog found himself more eager than before to see this expedition through.

They settled down for the night to the sounds of coyotes in the hills howling at the moon, in hopes that the silvery sphere might dull its bright light in order to make their presence less easily detectable to their prey. Or at least that was as logical an explanation as any for the canines' unpredictable behavior. The fire popped and crackled as it slowly burned itself out.

When Kelly awoke, shortly before dawn, he looked around the campsite and saw exactly what he expected to see: emptiness. Spotted Dog was well on his way, having left no sign that he had ever been there. Kelly smiled at the elusiveness of the red man as he gathered some juniper sticks and built up enough of a fire to get coffee started. His bag of Arbuckle's was being depleted more quickly than usual, since he was now brewing for two.

The campsite was still in the shadows. The full sun wouldn't reach over the peaks for another half hour or so. He could sit beneath the boulders and watch the road without suffering the heat of the full sun for some time. He drank his coffee and watched. A pair of hawks circled the flat desert, always on the lookout for a plump rodent for dinner. The road was devoid of travelers for as far as the eye could see. By midday there would be the daily wagon from the mine going to Desert Belle for supplies or delivering pieces of broken machinery to the blacksmith to repair. But he didn't expect any such commerce to pass by before noon. At night, wagons wouldn't travel the tricky road with its steep drop-offs on either side, gaping fissures appearing from washouts caused by sudden rains, or windblown debris or rocks that could split a wheel. While there had been no rains for days to cool down the stifling air, few things could change the travel plans of a mine's operator. Thus, he expected to see no wagons for another hour or so, since the mine was two hours away.

All he heard was the sound of a skittering pebble from behind him. Instantly alerted, he drew his Colt revolver and spun around. He came face-to-face with a grinning Apache. With a sigh, he slipped the .45 back into its holster.

"You want some coffee, old friend?" he said.

"I smell from long way off."

Kelly walked back to the campsite where the fire had waned but was sufficient to keep the coffee-pot hot. He poured a cup and handed it to the Indian, who accepted it with a gracious nod and a grunt of approval.

"Did you find where the man went?"

"No. His tracks not go to mine. Turn off into desert."

"So, he wasn't going to the mine, after all. Did you see anyone?"

"No."

"Well, he didn't come by here, so where could he have gotten off to?" Kelly scrunched up his mouth in thought, his long mustache brushing from side to side as if to sweep away any debris left from last night's tasty rabbit.

"There creek at bottom of hill beyond many boulders. Water running fast but shallow. Tracks lead into water but not come out."

"Either he figured he was being followed, or he decided not to take any chances."

Spotted Dog nodded and then slurped at the steaming cup.

"I reckon our choice has been made for us. No sense keeping our presence a secret anymore, if it was ever a secret in the first place. We'll have ourselves a visit with an old friend. Drink up. I'll douse these embers."

Kelly hadn't expanded on who the "old friend" might be. The Apache didn't really care, anyway, as he tried to always be ready for whatever might befall him. But if the lawman knew where he was going, that suited Spotted Dog just fine. Besides, there might be some more coffee at their destination. Hotter and tastier than the rather weak stuff Kelly had brewed up.

They passed the first warning signs that they'd arrived at a point that was considered by the property owners to be trespassing. This was a concept that the Apache could not understand, as it was known by all of his people that land could not be for only a few but must be open and free for all. At least, all Apaches. Or, more specifically, all Chiricahua.

The second set of signs, Kelly told him, were dire warnings that trespassers would be shot on sight. Spotted Dog asked, "How will they know we are not these trespassers?"

"Reckon we'll have to rely on our lucky rabbit's foot."

Spotted Dog shot him a questioning glance. "Apache not keep foot of those we eat."

"Well, in that case, we'll have to hope mine will cover us both." He chuckled as Spotted Dog gave him a brow-furrowing frown. "We'll be fine, unless things have changed more'n I imagine since my last visit."

The Apache was still unappreciative of Kelly's attempt at humor as they rode into the compound where several small buildings gathered to form the center of activity of the operation. Kelly smiled broadly as Molly McQueen, the manager, bounded down the steps of the mine manager's office.

"Land o'goshun. If it ain't my favorite lawman. Good to see you're still kickin'. Who's your friend?"

"Molly, this is Spotted Dog. He's helpin' me with some tracking. Best in the business, I reckon."

"Nice to meet'cha, Spotted Dog," she said.

The Indian returned her greeting with a nod.

"So, Marshal, who're you trackin'? Not one of my employees, I hope. Tough enough to keep 'em around long enough to earn their pay, let alone follow 'em into town every time they get a dollar to spend on liquor or such."

"Nope. We aren't lookin' for anyone who works

out here, but I am curious to know if a stranger, wearin high-top boots like mine and a brown felt hat, mighta ridden in late yesterday or this mornin' early."

Molly frowned thoughtfully, her gray hair a tangle as it framed an oval face that had seen many a hard time. "Nope. The only riders to come through them gates was those scoundrels, the Clutter brothers. Right nasty bunch they are too. Come lookin' for Pooder. Said they're holdin' paper in the amount of $100, and they looked like they intend to collect, one way or another."

"And I don't suppose you told them where they could find that young scalawag, did you?"

"If I'd known a lick about his comings and goings, I mighta been tempted to spill the beans. But as fate would have it, I ain't seen him since he rode off yesterday mornin' with a letter he was to mail for me. After he'd been gone a couple hours, Blue found the letter in the dirt right where that careless fool had dropped it. I sent Blue off to get it to the stage before it left. I hope to heavens he made it, 'cause if he didn't, I might as well turn in my bedroll and skedaddle outta these parts."

"I take it the letter was important."

"Life or death for this mine operation."

"I thought the mine was doing well."

"It was. Then, all of a sudden, we was in a hole almost too big to get out of. And gettin' bigger."

Chapter Fourteen

"Pooder, you ain't had a good idea since I met you. And it's lookin' more and more like you ain't goin' to, neither. Now, I made a promise to Miz Molly, and I intend to keep it. So, don't make me suffer through any more of your dimwitted 'great plans.' If you got a workable idea, say it. Otherwise, just shut up." Blue's fists were balled so tightly, his knuckles were turning—well, blue.

Pooder stared at his friend with his mouth agape. Blue had never jumped all over him like this before. Maybe it *was* time to step back and give the situation some serious thought. He had to admit—if only to himself—that his ideas of late hadn't had the benefit of his greatest deliberation. If he'd had more time to consider the problem, he was pretty sure he could come up with a truly exceptional plan, one that both he and Blue could accept. But first, he had to get Blue to calm down. Way down.

"Blue, my good and faithful friend, you know I wouldn't take one step toward doing anything that didn't sit right with you. So, what say we put our thoughts out where we can consider the alternatives, and then come to a sensible plan? A truly grand plan." Pooder took another step backward, eminently pleased with his conciliatory speech, especially since he didn't have to include anything about his maybe being a little foggy in his previous thinking on the matter.

Blue, on the other hand, wasn't buying Pooder's new attitude. He'd known the boy for almost two years now, and there wasn't a chance that he'd allow himself to be bamboozled by the pig farmer's silliness again, at least not anytime soon. And even if it meant risking life and limb, he was darned well going to see to it that Miz Molly's letter got to Tucson, one way or another. His eyes were narrowed, his jaw set. *Pooder better get the picture quick like, or I'm takin' off on my own.*

"Since there ain't no trains that come near Desert Belle, and the next stage ain't for quite a spell, and Miz Molly said this here letter had to be delivered in person, the only plan I see that has any chance of workin' is where we mount up and head for Tucson. Maybe we can get there shortly after the stagecoach, and things will still work out okay for the mine," Blue said.

"What do you mean, 'work out for the mine'? Is something wrong with the Lily?" Now it was Pooder's turn to get panicky. "We still got jobs, ain't we?"

"The look on Miz Molly's face when she said getting this letter to the stage in Desert Belle so it could get to Tucson fast was all I needed to know she wasn't just pennin' an account of her day's chores to her Aunt Tillie."

"I didn't even know she had an Aunt Tillie," Pooder blurted out. "She live in Tucson?"

"No, dummy. Molly don't have an Aunt Tillie. That's what you call a—oh, never mind. You wouldn't understand, anyway."

"Well, who is it with an Aunt Tillie?"

Blue's patience had reached a boiling point. *"Nobody has an Aunt Tillie, you idjit!* I was just making a point."

Pooder jumped at Blue's outburst. He scratched his head and mumbled something about being certain *someone* had an Aunt Tillie. But he knew better than to belabor the point. He'd never seen Blue like this before, right on the edge and looking to leap.

But as Pooder thought more about it, maybe going to Tucson wasn't such a bad idea, after all. It might get the Clutters off his back, for a little while at least. And maybe he could find a game that would make him the winner he knew he was capable of being. Then he could pay off those cardsharps and get free of their clutches. *Yep, sounds like Blue's on the right track.*

Besides, if he remembered right, about halfway to Tucson was a relay station that saw coaches going through all the time from different directions. That might be where they could find a line that went into Tucson and give the driver the letter to take the rest of the way. And a relay station was a good place to get a game of poker going with passengers looking to pass the time of day while the stationmaster changed horses and served up a meal.

"Blue, it's come to me clear as water. You're right. I'm all for us headin' for Tucson with the letter. And the sooner, the better too. Time's a'wastin', so let's gather a few vittles to take along and get saddled up."

Blue was startled by Pooder's sudden change of mind. But his quixotic friend had never been particularly easy to read. So, before the boy changed his mind and started blathering about some idea that had yet to see the light of day, Blue accepted and made a beeline for the general store. He figured that, under the circumstances, Miz Molly would forgive his charging a few necessities for the trip. She wouldn't want her employees to starve while on a mission to help save the mine from whatever disaster loomed.

At Carson's General Store and Mercantile, Blue hummed as he went about gathering some beans, coffee, peaches, bacon, flour, and a couple of canteens, which both boys had left the Lily without. Early the next morning, after a restless night sleeping on straw at the livery stable, the boys set out to make the trip to Tucson, their saddlebags stuffed to bulging like a pregnant cow. Quicksilver gave a disgruntled snort as Blue mounted up. Pooder's horse wasn't looking any more cooperative. They both must have sensed a long, hot ride somewhere.

"You sure you still got that letter, Blue? I don't want to get to our destination and find you left it on the counter at Carson's store." Blue groaned at his friend's lack of confidence, but that didn't keep him from checking his pocket just the same. He pulled the wrinkled and battered envelope out, turned it over, then refolded it and stuck it back and as far down in his pocket as he could. If he'd had a way to padlock it to his clothing, he would have.

"You bring a gun with you, Blue? In case we see a need to protect ourselves from road agents or Injuns?"

"Uh, no. I didn't expect to be travelin' all the way to Tucson, so I guess I come away unprepared for battle with the likes of Billy the Kid or some such. How about you? You always got a little pistol tucked down somewhere in your britches pocket or boot."

"Yeah, well, I also forget to bring along my little Colt, since I was thinkin' more of how much money I was goin' to take off them Clutters."

"Haven't you learned your lesson yet? The Clutters are thieves, card cheats, and swindlers. When you goin' to figure it out? You can't *never* win against them." Blue shook his head in disgust. Pooder might be a friend, but he sure was a lamebrain.

"I'm too good to be cheated. I'd know in an instant if a body was tryin' to pull a shady deal."

"I've seen you play. You're terrible. Why, I'll bet you don't even know what beats a full house," Blue said.

"I do too."

"Okay, what?"

"A straight. Or is it a flush? Maybe a straight flush. Yeah, that's it. See?"

Blue looked straight ahead, hoping Pooder would drift off the road, maybe drop into a hole and never come out. How could anyone be this dumb?

"You ain't sayin' nothin'."

"Got nothing to say. Just a lot of riding ahead of us. And I don't want to hear you blathering all the way."

"I sure wish there was another way to get the letter to Tucson. I surely do," Pooder moaned, his attention briefly diverted by a flash of light off to the west. Miles away, where the mountains were purple and deceivingly distant, a billowing thundercloud shot bolts of fire from its belly and brought rumbles rolling across the desert like cannon fire. He shuddered to think how he was soon going to be drenched to the skin. He had no slicker, and, as he glanced about, he saw no more protection from the approaching storm than they might find beneath a towering saguaro—which meant to say, none.

"Yeah. Too bad there ain't no trains going nearby." Blue also was looking to the west. He said nothing about what was obviously about to engulf them, but his concerns weren't without noting to himself that he wished Pooder had had the good sense to take care of Miz Molly's envelope and get it to the stage so everything would have worked out as planned. But no, this fool who never did anything right now had them in the middle of the desert with a gully-washer on its way.

Pooder chewed on that for several minutes before he lit up like one of those bolts of lightning. "That's it! That's the great plan! Blue, you may have saved the day."

Blue was shaken from his reverie. He looked over at Pooder as if the boy had lost his mind again or was about to blurt out another of his idiotic ideas, hoping to put it up for a vote. *It'll be a tie if he does, 'cause I've had all his nonsense I can handle for one day.*

But Zeb Pooder wouldn't be denied this time. His confidence was high, and he puffed out his chest and sat up straight.

"Blue, what you just said makes a lot of sense. I can't believe I didn't think of it before. You're a genius, that's what you are."

Blue knew when he was about to be handed

some horse hockey, but he chose not to scream, only look sideways with a narrow-eyed stare that he hoped would suggest to Pooder that he'd be better off to keep his harebrained ideas to himself. The look didn't deter his friend. Blue could but let out a sigh and brace himself. But he was about to get a shock.

"We'll be comin' to the Tombstone cutoff in a couple of hours. You know what that means?"

"I'll bet you're goin' to tell me, whether I want to hear or not. Ain't that true?"

"Yep. And you know why? 'Cause you're goin' to be dancin' with joy—uh, so to speak."

"Spit it out, Pooder. I ain't got all day, and I've got darned little patience."

"A train runs near Tombstone, and it goes all the way through to Tucson. I think it stops at Contention. Don't you see? We can put the letter on the train and not have to ride all the way to Tucson. It'll get there even faster."

Blue's face lit up. For once, Pooder had actually come up with a credible idea.

As soon as Blue and Pooder had turned the corner at the north edge of town and ridden out of Desert Belle, three disgruntled cardsharps strode down the street. Hank, Joe, and Bob Clutter headed straight for the Shot-to-Hell Saloon and a date with their next victim. The three had been fleecing all comers on a regular basis for almost six months, ever since they were driven out of Cochise by Sheriff John Henry Stevens and told never to return on pain of incarceration for some interminable time. Bob was in a bad mood after searching high and low in sweltering heat for Zeb Pooder and a chance to get the hundred dollars he was into them for.

"Quit your moping around, Bob; we'll get him sooner or later. Where could he hide that we couldn't ferret him out? Besides, truth be told, he don't owe us nothin', since we cheated him in the first place," Hank said, then laughed a deep belly laugh. Joe joined in. Finally Bob gave a sigh of resignation as they dismounted in front of the saloon. As he climbed the steps, Bob muttered something about he'd like to at least take a hunk out of the boy's hide just for the trouble.

"Would you settle for some fresh blood? Look over yonder at the gent coming outta the barber's chair. He looks flush and fat as a pig to market. Get out your hot decks, boys; things are about to get interestin'," Hank said.

"That fool kid was all but wiped out, anyway. Better we expand our clientele. I'm tired of reelin' in the small ones," Joe said, a greedy grin covering half his face.

Chapter Fifteen

"Think we can outrun that goose-drowner that's bearin' down on us?" Pooder asked.

"We still got a lot more miles to the Tombstone cutoff, so I'm bettin' against it," Blue said, looking over his shoulder with concern. "Would be nice to find us some shelter, though. Keep your eyes out for a cave or some boulders we can huddle under."

As the storm got closer, both boys were craning their necks every which way in hopes of finding some protection from what was about to overtake them. The wind picked up and swirled dirt and dust all around them. Then, just as a couple of lightning strikes hit so close they could feel the charged air on their skin, Pooder shouted that they'd better find a place of safety, and fast. Both dismounted in a rush to get somewhere less dangerous than the open. As they scrambled down into a gulley, tugging on the reins of their skittish horses, Blue spotted a craggy outcropping that looked as though it might offer some protection.

"There, Pooder, under them rocks."

They scampered down the side of the hill,

nearly losing their balance several times on the loose gravel. They quickly wrapped the reins of their mounts to a pathetic-looking willow tree and dove under a boulder that jutted out like a tongue. Just in time. The rain hit with such ferocity, they lost sight of their horses. Blue had ripped a hole in his britches, and Pooder had skinned both knees trying to gain purchase on the slippery climb to safety. They were puffing and panting, wiping water from their eyes, and cursing the evil storm gods for choosing them to torment. But that was only the beginning, as it turned out.

As the two of them sat beneath the overhang, soaked to the skin and shivering as the cold wind whipped around them, Blue couldn't help but speak up. "You know, if you hadn't dropped this here letter—"

Pooder held up a shaking hand. "Say no more. I know I am the cause of all our sorrow, and I repent. So you can set me free from the clutches of everlasting guilt. I've paid my dues."

"Reckon it depends on whether we get to Contention in one piece," Blue mumbled.

The rain persisted for more than an hour, an unusually long time for a sudden, late-summer storm. But they knew the worst of it was over when there came just the slightest hint of yellow in the boiling sky. The wind, too, had lost some of its bite. A warmer, friendlier wind seemed about to reach them. Then, almost as suddenly as it started, those plump droplets of moisture shrank nearly to nothing. Blue let out a "Whew!" and commenced to crawl out from under the rocks. His back was aching from being jammed so far underneath them, he thought he'd never be able to stand up straight again.

They dragged their soaked bodies free and began to retrace their steps to where they had tied their mounts. "Uh-oh, Pooder, ain't that the tree I tied Quicksilver to? And your horse with it?"

"That's the one. Only thing is, them cayuses ain't there no more. What do you suppose could have happened?" Pooder shielded his eyes from the glare of the sun, then turned around and around to examine the desert. "Hey, there's some tracks. Maybe they spooked and ran to that dry creek bed down there."

"That ain't good. They could get swept away by the rushing water that'll surely be comin' down from the mountains. We best get a move on before it's too late."

They both bounded down the incline in search of their mounts. When Blue spotted Quicksilver, she was peacefully grazing in a patch of grass that still had slight tinges of green. Pooder's horse was several yards away, standing still as if on guard for some impending danger. At that moment, Quicksilver also was moved to rear her head in the same direction. Blue looked off to see if he could detect what the horses were engrossed in. That's when he yelled.

"Pooder! Look! The waters are comin' fast. Get the horses uphill, or we'll lose 'em."

The two broke into a dead run for the horses, which, after considering such a move, hadn't been exactly the right thing to do. It spooked the horses, and instead of running away from the oncoming flood of muddy, fast-moving rain-water, they ran farther into its path. The boys picked up their pace. Pooder was waving his arms and calling his horse every name he could think of, but, unfortunately, not being conversant in mangled English, the horse understood not a word.

Blue got within a few feet of Quicksilver, but the horse shied away just out of reach, causing the boy to make a fruitless dive into the now-soggy ground. But Blue, ever optimistic, scrambled to his feet and charged after the horse. Getting close enough to almost feel her breath, he made a last lunge at the dangling reins. Aha! Quicksilver yanked her head away but a little too late. Blue had a firm grip on one of the reins and was hanging on for dear life. The frightened horse pulled and pulled, her eyes wide with terror, dragging Blue across the gravelly desert as if he were no more than a pesky mutt that needed to be taught a lesson. The horse soon tired sufficiently for Blue to grab the second rein, and, that done, he was able to get Quicksilver under control. By the time he was able to clamber into the saddle, soaked to the skin, muddy, and looking as if he'd been stomped by a herd of buffalo, Blue turned the horse around and urged her to where Pooder was having no luck at all corralling his mount. Blue caught the errant horse and led it back to his friend, whose exasperation was clearly getting the best of him.

Puffing and panting, Pooder growled, "Thanks for saving this worthless bag of bones. I reckon I wasn't all that thrilled at the prospect of walkin' to Tombstone, or, for that matter, ridin' double."

"You're welcome. And likewise, I'm sure. Now, let's get ourselves and these dumb animals out of the way of that wall of water I see comin' fast."

Digging their heels into their horse's flanks, they made it to high ground not a second too soon. The roiling waters were as dark as the sky had been at the height of the storm, carrying with it all manner of debris and unfortunate desert critters.

"There goes my hat," Pooder whined, pointing to a sad-looking piece of soggy felt that had already seen better days but was now about to reach a pitiful end, jammed into some muddy crevice or ripped apart on cactus barbs.

"Yeah, well, I lost mine on the way to town, so now we're even," Blue said, still trying to catch his breath. "Best we get a move on. We're wastin' time worryin' about hats and such."

It was several hours before they reached the turnoff to Tombstone and Contention City. A worn wooden marker pointed the way. But Pooder and Blue found they were no longer alone on the trail, for as they approached the marker, they were surprised to see a man leaning against it, his hat tilted forward to shade his eyes or take a nap, neither boy was sure. The man's horse was grazing nearby.

"Howdy, mister. You headed for Tombstone?" Pooder said, as Blue frowned at him for giving away their destination to a stranger who had no business knowing.

The man tilted his hat back on his head. "Why, hello, boys. Yep, reckon that's my destination. Figured a little siesta wouldn't hurt none. Besides, bein' out in the heat of day tires me."

"Didn't you get caught in that storm that went by?"

"It passed farther to the south. Didn't mean much to me. Say, you fellas mind if I ride along with you? Since we're all goin' the same direction, I could use the company."

"Naw. We don't mind. You're welcome to ride along," Pooder volunteered.

Again Blue shot Pooder a "shut your flapping mouth" look, which didn't register with the verbose pig farmer. Blue shook his head in disgust, knowing full well that whatever he said or did would not register one iota with Pooder.

"It's gettin' on time to rustle up some grub and have a little siesta. You boys got any extra food with you?"

The forward gent's conversation had already gotten Pooder to tell him where they were headed, and now Blue would bet every penny of his next paycheck that Pooder would agree to share anything he and Blue had, without ever considering consulting his partner in this venture. He shook his head knowingly at Pooder's next words.

"Why, mister, we'd be happy as larks to make you our guest. Never let it be said that Zebulan Pooder ever turned a hungry man away."

"Thank you kindly, son. You're my kind of traveling companion."

And now this owlhoot even knows Pooder's name. I don't believe it.

"Looks like a handy place to set up camp over beyond that stand of mesquite and willows. If I remember right, there's a pool of clean water right in the middle of it." The man led out, and Pooder dutifully followed, giving no thought whatsoever to consulting Blue, who turned Quicksilver to fall in, knowing any objection would be futile.

When they got to the low spot where several

trees clung tenaciously to the edge of a shallow pool of greenish water, the man dismounted, motioning for the boys to do the same.

"Why don't one of you boys gather a few pieces of deadfall, and we'll build ourselves a fire? What did you bring along to eat?"

Blue jumped in before Pooder could spill the beans, so to speak. "Why, we got some coffee, and I found a can of beans before we left town. That ought to hold us until we reach our destination." He gave Pooder a "don't you dare open your mouth" look that stung the boy into silence.

"That sounds good, boys. I'll just take another little nap until I smell the coffee a-bubblin'."

Later, after the coffee had been downed and every last bean found its way into someone's stomach, the stranger sighed and then turned serious.

"So, boys, you ever hear of a mine over near Desert Belle called the Gilded Lily?"

"Why, sure, we work there," Pooder blurted out, giving absolutely no thought to any possible consequences.

"That right? You know a fella name of Abner Dillard?"

"Of course. Didn't I just say we work there? Everybody knows Abner. He's the clerk, or something like that." Pooder looked down as he realized he had no idea what Abner's job entailed. "How do you know Mr. Dillard?"

"He's a good friend. Known him for quite a spell. Say, you never did say what you're doin' goin' to Tombstone," said the man.

Pooder shot off his mouth again before Blue could shut him up. "We ain't actually goin' to Tombstone. We got to make it to Contention City so we can put an important letter onto the train to Tucson. We got it right here."

"Well, since I'm going that direction on business, there don't seem to be any good reason why we all three should make the trip. What say you give me the letter, and I'll see to it that it gets on that mail train?"

"Uh, no, sir, we couldn't do a thing like that," Blue said, his brow wrinkled at the stranger's plan.

"Well, actually, that wasn't exactly a suggestion. It was an order. Hand that letter over, and do it now, if you know what's good for you."

Both boys' eyes went wide with surprise. Even though Blue had had little trust of this stranger from the beginning, he hadn't expected to be held up. He didn't move a muscle as the man's hand slipped down to his six-shooter and eased it out. He cocked it as he pointed it at the boys.

"Don't make me do something I'd rather not do. I want that letter, and I want it right now!"

"Better give it to him, Blue. Ain't no sense gettin' shot over a piece of paper."

The man moved toward Blue and aimed the

revolver right at his head. "Your friend is givin' you good advice, boy. *Now!*"

Scared nearly out of his mind, Blue shot a hand into his pocket to retrieve the letter. That's when the real shock came. His pocket was empty. The letter was gone.

Chapter Sixteen

Kelly was mulling over what Molly had told him about the three men who'd come looking for Pooder. "Molly, tell me more about these Clutter brothers. How long have they been around Desert Belle?"

"About six months, if memory serves. They hang around the saloons lookin' for suckers like Pooder to fall into their trap. Then they cheat 'em blind and afterward make sure they got some paper on 'em so they can hound them till they drop . . . or run. A bad bunch, they are."

"Why hasn't the sheriff run them out of town?"

"Hawk Burns? That mouthy pile of horse dung! Why, he wouldn't stick his nose outside that office of his if there was the least danger he could get it blown off."

"Hawk Burns. Yeah, we met him earlier. What do you know about him?"

"Been around. Kansas, Nebraska, Texas, New Mexico—you name it, he's been hired and fired everywhere he's been. A fellow with no backbone don't last long out here, or haven't you noticed? He tries to look dangerous, but he ain't."

Kelly thought about that for a moment, then told Molly to look him up if Pooder didn't come back. He said he'd keep an eye out for him in town. He asked if there was a message she wanted relayed.

"Yeah. Tell him he can pick up his bedroll and scoot on out of here. Maybe some other operation wouldn't mind wet-nursin' a half-growed idjit." She turned and stomped off toward the office. Just the mention of Pooder's name seemed to have ruined her morning. Kelly shrugged and motioned for Spotted Dog to mount up.

As they reached the first gate, they met up with a guard wielding a twelve-gauge shotgun. He was lighting a match to a just-rolled cigarette. Kelly reined in, leaning on the saddle horn.

"Howdy. Didn't see you when we came through about a half hour ago."

"I was, er, off in the sticks, uh—"

"Never mind. I got the picture. Say, pardner, did you happen to see a fellow hangin' around late yesterday or early this mornin'? He's got a pair of boots like mine and wears a brown felt hat."

The man seemed to be searching his memory as he slowly responded. "Can't rightly recall seein' no one of that description; just them ornery Clutters come by yesterday. Sorry."

Kelly touched the brim of his Stetson and said, "Thanks."

The two continued on their way back to Desert Belle.

"Show me where our man left the road."

Spotted Dog grunted and took the lead. After almost a half hour, he pulled up, pointing to a set of recent tracks beside the road. The lone rider appeared to have waited briefly, smoking a cigarette before heading out cross-country to the north.

"I sure do wonder what that fellow was doin' out this way. And what connection our man might have to the Gilded Lily."

As they rode, the desert was alive with sounds of birds. They flitted and dove, in and out of saguaro apartments or into rocky ledges. A sleek-coated coyote wandered out from behind a creosote bush, stopped and nonchalantly looked Kelly over for a second, then turned his steely gaze to Spotted Dog, which brought about a quick retreat into the relative safety of a thick cactus colony. That brought a smile to Kelly's normally serious lips. *Reckon more than just the settlers have a healthy respect for the Apache.*

When they got back to Desert Belle, Kelly was faced with a dilemma. He needed to stay around town for a while to see if their man came back. But he knew if he tried to put Spotted Dog up in the hotel, he'd have problems. He couldn't be sure whether the hotel manager or the Apache would be the more obstinate about the arrangement. Finally, he decided he'd ask the liveryman to put them both up for the night. When he'd spoken to the liveryman before, he hadn't noticed any of the usual fear and loathing apparent when someone came face-to-face with a Chiricahua— the tribe of Cochise and Geronimo, two of the most feared men on the frontier. Besides, if the man went along with Kelly's idea, it would help out his expense account for the month. His expenditures had been running a little higher than usual, and he wanted to save up to wine and dine Nettie at the hotel back in Cochise—mostly to get her out of her own kitchen. And it would be worth every penny, even having to listen to the claptrap he'd surely get from the government paymaster.

The liveryman accepted a reasonable daily rate to put the two of them up in a couple of seldom-used stalls near the rear door. After getting their horses fed and put away, Kelly told the Apache he'd return soon. He wanted to revisit the sheriff, hoping to tap into information he might have about the Clutters and the rumors of crooked gambling.

"We'll round up some grub when I get back," he said.

The Apache grunted and squatted on the straw, leaning back against the rails. Kelly wasn't certain why he worried about the Apache's welfare, but he did. It nagged at him. He'd seen what the citizens of a town were capable of when someone who didn't look or act like them was in their midst. It only took a few shots of whiskey for a man to build up an unhealthy dose of courage, and then the trouble would begin. Almost always, someone got hurt. He didn't want that someone to be Spotted Dog.

When he got to the jail, he looked in through the window before trying the door. The sheriff was not inside. He decided he'd go to the Shot-to-Hell Saloon. There he might just rub elbows with the Clutters and get a chance to see for himself what some seemed to consider the scourge of the town.

It didn't take him long to spot the three gamblers. They had two suckers seated with them, and they were loud and obnoxious. The sheriff was leaning on the bar, engaged in a conversation with a couple of cowboys. Kelly eased up to the bar and ordered a beer. Tossing his dime onto the oak surface, he turned to watch the Clutter brothers work their crooked play on the unsuspecting gents. One of the men was definitely not a cowboy, and he didn't look as if he was from town, either. His clothes were dusty, as if he'd ridden some distance to get there. Kelly turned to the bartender.

"Say, who are those three fellows who look like brothers?" he asked the bar keep.

"That's the Clutters. Hank's the big one in the middle, then Joe to his left, and Bob's the skinny one."

"Who is that gentleman in the sack suit playing cards at the table near the wall?"

The bartender squinted, then said, "That's just a whiskey drummer who came in on the stage yesterday."

"He sell you anything?"

"Some. He's from Kentucky. They make a fine bourbon there."

"Do you figure those boys are runnin' a straight game?"

"I don't know. I never gamble, myself. I know my limitations. I will say, they sure are a lucky bunch. They walk out of here flush near every day."

"People ever complain to the sheriff about being cheated?"

"Sure. But, if they do, ain't nothin' gettin' done about it. The sheriff said he's looked in on 'em several times, but he ain't spotted any cheatin'."

"Maybe they clean it up when he's around."

"Could be. Want another beer?"

"No thanks. I think I'll stroll over there and watch that game for a spell."

Kelly pulled his vest closed and buttoned it to cover his badge. The sheriff hadn't acknowledged his presence yet. Maybe if the Clutters didn't know who he was, they would tip their hand. As he sauntered up, Hank Clutter looked at him briefly. "Lookin' to sit in, mister?"

"Maybe later. Thought I'd watch for a minute or two."

"Can't say I like the idea of some hombre lookin' over my shoulder while I work. Never know when a fella might be passin' signals or somethin'. You understand?"

"Sure. Of course, if you were dealin' off the bottom or workin' a shaved deck, I can see why you wouldn't want onlookers, cither."

That hit a nerve with Hank Clutter. He stood up with fire in his eyes, dumped his chair over backward, and his hand went to the butt of his revolver.

"You callin' me a cheat, mister? Not many ever done that and lived."

Kelly held up a hand in conciliation. "Now hold on, pardner. No one's accusin' you of anything. Just like to know a game's fair and square before I sit down, that's all. Sorry you got the wrong impression."

Hank seemed to settle down a bit. He took his hand away from his gun and bent over to retrieve his chair. He eased down slowly, never taking his eyes off the tall stranger.

"Well, okay, but if I see you makin' signs at any of these fellas, I'll plug you where you stand. Understand?"

"I'm not here to cause you any bother, mistcr.

Just decidin' if I want to sit in." Kelly hooked his thumbs over his gun belt and stood nonchalantly looking on. Every once in a while Hank would look his way but would return quickly to watching the other players' faces for signs of a bad hand. The whiskey drummer didn't appear to be having a very good day. His pile of money was pitifully small to be in a game with four other players.

After several minutes, the sheriff, who had overheard the earlier exchange between the marshal and Hank Clutter, wandered over, tapped Kelly on the shoulder, and motioned him aside. They walked to the door, and Hawk Burns led the way outside.

"I couldn't help overhearin' what you said to Hank. I don't know what you've heard, but them boys play an honest game. Why, I've stood over them a dozen times and never caught even a sleight of hand. They're just darned good with the pasteboards, that's all."

"Well, Sheriff, I reckon I'm bound to take your word for it. However, in the few minutes I stood there, the one to Hank's left palmed a card, and Hank, himself, dealt twice off the bottom of the deck. Now, I will grant you that they are very shrewd gamblers, but it really isn't in the town's best interest to condone that caliber of card-sharp."

Sheriff Burns' expression turned dour, and Kelly could see the heat building inside him.

"Listen, Marshal, this here is *my* town, and I take responsibility for seein' to it that folks hereabouts arc trcatcd fair. I never heard where a U.S. Marshal was charged with watchin' over gamblin' activities. So I'm figuring this is out of your jurisdiction. Am I right?"

Kelly puzzled over that for a moment, knowing that a run-in with the sheriff at this time could compromise other things he was looking into.

"Right you are, Sheriff. I'll be careful not to make out I know what the Clutters arc pullin' on the citizens of this fair town. But if I hear of any of *my* friends bein' taken, I might have to change my mind. I'd say you oughta watch them boys a little closer. As you say, it's *your* town."

Sheriff Burns bristled at Kelly's warning. With his eyes narrowed and fists balled, he spun on his heel and marched across the street and up a block to the jail. Kelly smirkcd with more than a touch of self-satisfaction as he watched Burns disappear into the adobe building and slam the door behind him.

Deciding it was time to check on Spotted Dog, he went back down to the livery. When he got to the rear stall where the two of them were to spend the night, the Apache was nowhere in sight. He called to the liveryman and was met by a young boy with a rake peering around a corner.

"Excuse me, son, do you know where the Indian that came in here has gone?"

"Sure, mister. I saw him climb onto that pony of his and hightail it out of town about a half hour ago."

"Which way did he go? And did he say anything before he left?"

"He headed west out thataway. He didn't say nothin', but he took off right after some other feller rode out."

Kelly hurriedly began saddling his gelding.

Chapter Seventeen

A mile outside of Desert Belle, Kelly saw Spotted Dog approaching from the other direction. He reined in until the Apache rode up.

"I hear you rode out after some fellow left the saloon."

"Don't know about that. I have need to see if man we follow double back to town. I no see tracks."

"I watched those gamblers at work. Didn't look like anyone except them was havin' a good day at the tables. If Molly's right about Zeb Pooder, it seems he wasn't the only one around here losin' money to the Clutters." As he considered the mine, Kelly began thinking back on things he'd found in Alex Bond's house. Papers, mostly, and not any of interest, except one that suggested he sought an interest in the Gilded Lily Mine. "It's beginning to look like our mysterious stranger may be Alex Bond, after all."

The Apache didn't know what the marshal was muttering about, so he just sat astride his pony and patiently awaited their next move.

"I need to send a telegram to Sheriff Stevens —see if he can give us a description of this Bond.

At least that might tell us who we're looking for. Then all we need to know is how or why he felt the need to kill those three bounty hunters. If, indeed, he did."

They rode back to town side by side. When they got to the livery, Kelly told the Apache to go inside and wait for him to return with some food.

Spotted Dog nodded and grinned. "Coffee too?"

"Coffee too." Kelly laughed as he rode off toward a café at the other end of town. As he got closer, an idea came to him. *I remember some great food being served when I stayed at Mrs. Dunham's. I wonder if she'd agree to my buying some steaks and fresh bread to take down to the livery.* When he was recuperating from a gunshot to the back the last time he was in town, lying in his iron bed at Mrs. Dunham's, he could still remember the mouthwatering smells drifting upstairs of fresh bread baking in the oven.

He turned to go up the hill on Galt Street. Mrs. Dunham's house stood at the end, near a cliff that dropped off steeply to a skirt of small boulders below. The same cliff wound around behind the jail and had figured prominently in the Bishop brothers' escape a year earlier. He dismounted and started up the stairs to Mrs. Dunham's wide porch. He was instantly reminded of her mouthwatering homemade biscuits. As he was about to knock, Hank Clutter yanked the door open and pointed a gun at him. Kelly heard footsteps behind him. He looked around to see the other two Clutter brothers coming up the steps.

"What's your business, here, Mr. *Marshal?*"

"How did you know I'm a marshal?"

"I got friends."

"Maybe a sheriff?"

"What're you suggesting?"

"Nothing, really. Just that in your line of work, it would certainly be helpful to have a lawman for a friend."

"And what do you figure my line of work might be?"

"I figure the three of you make a fair living off your gambling profits."

"There something wrong with that?"

"Nope. Not as long as it's an honest game."

"That's the second time you've hinted that we're not straight shooters. That how you feel? And what would be your proof?"

"I have no *evidence* to suggest that you are anything other than what you say you are."

"Hmph." Hank put his gun back into its holster and stepped back from the door. "Come on in, *Marshal*. Mrs. Dunham's out back. I reckon that's who you came to see, ain't it?"

"That's correct, Mr. Clutter." Kelly tipped his hat to Hank and strode past him, giving his arm a nudge as he brushed by. He was pretty sure he heard Hank snarl, just a little. But he didn't look back to see any reaction.

He walked straight through the house, down the long hallway to the back, where the kitchen was. He could hear the clatter of pans as Mrs. Dunham busied herself with cooking the next meal. When he entered the door to the kitchen, he knocked on the frame to let her know she had a visitor.

Her eyes lit up as she recognized him. "Why, Marshal Piedmont Kelly! What a delight. You been away so long, I feared somethin' bad might have happened to you."

"No, ma'am. As you can see, I'm still in one piece."

"What brings you back to Desert Belle? You still keepin' an eye on them two mischievous rascals that near got themselves shot up by outlaws?"

"No, although I thought I might look them up, see how they're doin'. I'm trying to find a man. Tall, slender, and wearin' stovepipe boots like mine. He also wears a floppy brown felt hat, I'm told. Don't suppose you've seen him."

"Nope. Sorry."

"I didn't figure you had. But I've got another request. I'm travelin' with a friend, and we're stayin' overnight down at the livery. I wondered if you'd be willin' to sell me some dinner for the two of us. Maybe for a couple of days."

"How come you're staying at the livery? I still rent out rooms, you know."

"Well, my friend might not sit too well with your other guests."

"Oh? Is he sickly, disfigured? Something like that to frighten a body?"

"No, he's a Chiricahua Apache scout, and a mighty fine one, at that."

"Oh," Mrs. Dunham said, placing a hand to her mouth. She chewed on that information for a minute, then decided the marshal had a pretty good reason for staying at the livery. She tried to hide her fear of the Indians, but it was impossible to conceal it from a man with Kelly's years of experience reading faces. "Well, you can count on me to gather you some dinner. If you can wait a few minutes, I'll bundle up a real nice feed for you. I don't suppose there are any special foods, uh, your friend won't eat, uh, or are there? I mean, he ain't expectin' grubs or snake or some weird—"

"I can tell you for certain, ma'am, that he wouldn't turn up his nose at anything you come up with, as long as it includes lots of hot coffee," Kelly said with a chuckle.

"Oh, my. Likes coffee, does he? Hee-hee," she chortled. "You go on, Marshal, and I'll send Johnny down to the livery with your dinner soon as it's ready."

"Johnny?"

"My nephew. He came from back east to live with me when his mother died of a fever last winter. You'll like him; he's a good boy." As she tottered on back to her chores, Kelly went past the parlor to the front door. When he got to the porch, two of the Clutters were gone. One was sitting on the porch railing, spitting tobacco into the flower bed. *Mrs. Dunhan'd likely take a broom to him if she knew what he was doing,* Kelly thought as he passed without a word.

He strolled down the street toward the livery. He took his time, stopping occasionally to peer into a window or chat briefly with someone sitting on a bench along the way. He almost got swept away by an apron-wearing lady who was more interested in ridding her store of the dirt tracked in by customers than being on the look-out for where the dirt, and her broom, were aimed. "Oh, my goodness. I'm so sorry. I wasn't aware that anyone might be there."

Kelly tipped his hat, said there was no apology necessary, and continued on his way. In front of the barbershop, a clean-shaven man stepped from the door, stopped to take a deep breath of air, then straightened his vest and walked away. The smell of rosewater hung in the air as he passed by. Kelly unconsciously rubbed his chin. The barber turned his OPEN sign around to say CLOSED. *Too late now to think about grooming this scratchy face.*

As he walked up the slight incline into the livery, he had a strange feeling of being followed. He hadn't noticed anyone who appeared sus-

picious, nothing overt; it was more like the feeling a man gets when a rifle is being pointed at
him by someone in hiding. It was instinctive. The
skin tingles, even when one can see neither hide
nor hair of the triggerman. Kelly tightened his
grip on his ever-present Winchester carbine.

When he reached the stalls at the back, Spotted
Dog was staring out the wide-open rear doors at
the corral, seemingly deep in thought. "Food is on
its way," Kelly said as he eased onto a bale of
straw with a sigh. The Indian grunted, never losing
his concentration. Kelly decided not to engage
him in frivolous conversation, aware that words
between men needn't at all times be forth-
coming. He settled back to his own reverie. He
thought back to his father, a minister who had
been shot down as he tried to protect a woman
from gunmen during the course of a robbery.

When Kelly was growing up, whenever his father
entered a room, someone had to volunteer to talk,
or he was chastised as being too private, too
withdrawn. The Reverend Jedediah Kelly was a
man of words, and they flowed freely whenever he
had someone to talk to. Kelly admired his father, a
man of principle, but he was also one who could
put you to sleep with his sermonizing. The young
Kelly was expected to go to school to become a
pastor like his father. Young men followed in their
father's footsteps; it was the proper thing to do.
But after the elder Kelly's death, Piedmont vowed

to seek justice through other means: as a lawman. To this day, he never wavered from, nor doubted the validity of, his decision. He also refrained from talking a great deal.

Within a few minutes, they heard a young voice calling from the front door. "Marshal Kelly, you in here?"

"Back here, son, near the rear doors."

A skinny, towheaded sprout about ten years of age hurried toward them toting a box. Kelly took the box from the boy, thanked him, and set the box down. As soon as the boy saw Spotted Dog emerge from the shadows, his eyes grew wide, and he hightailed it out of the livery so fast, he almost sucked all the air out of the room. Kelly chuckled at the boy's reaction to seeing a real, live Apache up close enough to touch. Clearly, the boy's education had been lacking in matters of frontier life.

The Indian saw no humor in it. He set immediately to finding something to eat.

Kelly hadn't exaggerated the quality of Mrs. Dunham's cooking. Spotted Dog ignored the utensils provided, grabbed up a piece of steak, and was gnawing on it before Kelly could look away to keep from breaking out into laughter. He, instead, carefully forked out a steak for himself, placed it on a tin plate, and commenced to slice it into bite-sized chunks. As he ate, Spotted Dog finally spoke up.

"White man has many things come between him and his hunger." He gave Kelly a wry grin, which the lawman interpreted as a lesson in the art of dining.

After eating, Kelly leaned back against a rail, tilted his Stetson, and was soon fast asleep. He'd been asleep no more than an hour, when he was awaked by a sound. He sat up, trying to adjust his eyes to the darkness, then eased himself to the hallway side of the stall. He retrieved his rifle and cocked it. Trying to be as quiet as possible, and seeing that Spotted Dog was not where he had placed his blankets, he stepped carefully to the door to the corral. Only his gelding and the Indian's pony were there. Then he heard the sound again: a muffled groan.

He stepped outside to see if he could determine from where the sound had originated. Suddenly, Spotted Dog stood up from behind a pile of straw and manure. Kelly squinted to see what was going on. The Apache had a man by the collar and was dragging him across the dirt. The man was limp, possibly unconscious. As the Indian came closer, Kelly could see that the man was Joe Clutter, the youngest of the Clutter brothers, and the one who had been lounging on Mrs. Dunham's porch as Kelly left there.

There was blood on Joe's shirt. And from the look of him, Kelly was pretty certain he was no longer alive.

Chapter Eighteen

Blue was sure he would pee his pants if the gravel-voiced man kept waving that .45 in his face and making all manner of threats to his continued welfare. Pooder was no help at all, as he could only sputter and try to come up with an explanation for the letter's being missing.

"Quit your dancin' around, kid," the man said to Pooder. "Either hand over the letter, or say your prayers. You got two minutes."

"But I told you, we don't have it. Blue musta lost it outta his pocket when we was almost washed away in that flood back there and drowned. I'm not tellin' no fib, mister. It's gone. I swear it is." Pooder was nearly frantic that the stranger would blow them both away and there wasn't a thing either of them could do about it.

"Where did you have it?"

"I-It was in m-my shirt pocket, right here." He tugged open his pocket to show it was empty.

"Take off your drawers, and do it now!" The man was becoming more and more insistent that they had the letter but were trying to bluff him.

Blue stood dumbfounded for a moment before the look on the man's face convinced him that cooperation was the only chance he had to live to see his next birthday. He began hopping around on one foot while he pulled off one brogan, then the other. When he was finally able to stand still, his pants fell down around his knees, then dropped in a heap at his feet.

"Kick 'em over here, kid, and do it now!"

He did as he was ordered. The stranger picked up the pants and began checking the pockets. When he found no sign of any letter, he threw the pants back in Blue's face and turned his attention to Pooder.

"Now you."

"M-Me?" sputtered Pooder.

"Yes, you. You're the mouthy one. The one with all the answers."

Pooder did as he was told, although not as quickly as the man expected until the barrel of the revolver in the man's hand inched closer and closer to his ear. That's when first the boots, then the pants, came off in a hurry. He tossed them at his detractor, who caught them with a snarl. The man went through the same routine, finally throwing them to the ground and giving them a kick. The pants landed on top of a prickly-pear cactus. The boys stood half naked, wondering what was about to befall them. The man lowered his weapon and turned around, kicking at a clump of dirt and cursing. He stopped and turned back to them with a face twisted in anger. "All right, you two are going to take me back to where you were when the storm hit. And you'd better find the right spot. Or else."

The boys started for their horses. The man shouted, "And get your damned pants on!"

Blue grabbed his and struggled to get a leg through after the man had all but turned them inside out. The cuff was tangled up in his pocket. He finally succeeded. He yanked on the little ear at the back of his brogan and pulled one on and then the other. But Pooder had been so knotted up with fear, trying to get the right leg into the right hole seemed to be only the latest in a series of bumbles. When he finally slipped into his second boot and stood up, he found he had put his pants on backward. He looked at the man who was glaring at him with such animosity, he decided that backward was no worse than not at all. He climbed into the saddle and tried to ignore his discomfort. He knew if he lived through this day, Blue would never let him live this moment down.

As they rode, the sun was bearing down on them with blistering intensity, and neither boy had a hat. Blue was mopping at his brow with first one shirtsleeve and then the other, both of which were now sopping wet. Pooder couldn't keep the perspiration out of his eyes no matter what he tried, and he kept blinking like a toad in a hailstorm. He had trouble even making out where they were headed. He was so uncomfortable, with his twisted, backward pants pinching him in unspeakable places, he had grown to really not much care whether he got shot or not.

After an hour's ride, the stranger yelled, "Where the hell is it? You boys better not be leading me around in circles. If you don't find the spot quick like, by damn you'll be tomorrow's pickin's for the buzzards."

Blue and Pooder both were swinging their gaze from side to side like nervous quail with a coyote in the vicinity. Blue tried to think back to the place where they'd hunkered down below the outcropping of boulders, but with the rain pelting them and the wind howling and peppering them with dirt, and them scrambling to find cover, he wasn't sure he could remember the place if he was standing next to it. Pooder was so caught up in worrying about his pants, he wasn't even looking anymore. The fear rising in Blue's throat made him feel sick. He was almost to the point of daring the man to shoot, so he could welcome death.

Just then, the outcropping came into view. It was twenty yards off to their left, and the dry wash wandered aimlessly below, at the bottom of a hill. Suddenly, it all came back. This was definitely where they had had trouble catching their horses. This place had to be where the letter came loose and was likely just lying there waiting to be found. He prayed so hard, his head hurt.

"There! That's the place. Down that hill and across the wash." Blue stood up in his stirrups and pointed downhill and across the wash.

"Get off your horses. We'll go on foot," the stranger ordered.

As they dismounted, a terrible thought came to Blue. When his horse was dragging him across the gravel, and the water was rushing toward them, and the wind was whipping up a terrific blow, what chance was there that the letter had stayed put? The darned thing could be in Mexico by now! *And we're about to be shot.* He felt his face turn ashen as reality overtook him.

"Point to where we're goin'!" shouted the man.

Hesitantly, Blue aimed a shaky finger to where he remembered trying to recapture his skittish horse. "Somewhere over there, across the wash." And then he added, under his breath so only Pooder could hear, "I hope."

The man led the way, ordering them to stay close behind him. They tried to comply, but Pooder's pants were becoming an awful nuisance, and halfway down the slippery gravel incline, he tripped, lost his balance, and went plunging forward. He crashed into the man, sending him head over heels into a many-armed and lethal teddy bear cholla. The sting of the cactus barbs driving deep into his flesh caused the man to scream. He dropped his gun in a last ditch effort to keep from hitting the deadly desert pincushion straight on by twisting his lanky body sideways. He almost succeeded, but as fate would have it, his arm went through the cactus as he hit the ground. He tried rolling away, but in doing so, he hit his head on a large rock half-buried in the sand. Blood ran down his hair and onto the sandy wash. The man was out cold.

Seeing the first opportunity to save themselves since meeting up with the vile stranger, Blue grabbed the gun, holding it in a shaking hand. The man began moaning, but his eyes remained shut.

"Get to your horse, Pooder. Now's our chance to get clean away from this owlhoot." Blue was waving the gun around, and Pooder kept ducking so that if it went off accidentally, he wouldn't end up as the target.

"Hey, watch where you're aiming that thing. I don't want my ears shot off."

"Then get a move on, or I *will* shoot you. If it hadn't been for your stupidity, we wouldn't be in this mess, and you know it." Blue finally stuck the Remington into his belt.

They started scrambling for the top of the rise where their horses had been left. The gravel was loose, and for every three steps forward, they'd slide back one. They finally reached the top without looking back.

"Let's take his horse with us. That way he'll

never catch us, and we can get back to Desert Belle and tell the sheriff," Blue said. Then he thought better of it. Leaving a man afoot in the desert was plain murder.

Pooder was still struggling with his backward pants, but he managed to mumble something about that just slowing them down. They were mounted and urging their mounts to a run when they heard the stranger yelling and cursing them. They knew that if he were to somehow catch up to them, they'd be nothing but bleached bones before anyone found their bodies.

"Oh, no," Pooder moaned.

"What?" Blue said without really caring whatever it was that Pooder found regretful.

"We *should* have taken his horse with us. Now he can come after us. We could still be dead as a rock."

"I got his gun. I don't think he'll be too eager to find out if I got the guts to pull the trigger on him." Blue patted the butt of the Remington. If he had to shoot this man who had threatened them with the same fate, he knew he could do it. He'd shot a man before, and with no remorse.

They kept up the fast pace as long as they could. But before too long, both horses were lathered up and heaving from the heat. They reined in and began walking the horses to cool them down.

"We got to find water. These horses won't make

it to town if they don't get a drink," Blue said.

"Yeah, but we don't know this country. We don't even know where to start looking for water."

Just then Blue saw some sandstone cliffs off to their right. At the top was a forest of saguaro cacti. Mesquite, paloverde, and brittlebush hugged the thin topsoil all the way to the bottom. "Let's head for those cliffs. They might just have some pools where water has collected. All that green stuff growin' up the sides must be gettin' water from somewhere."

Blue dismounted and began leading Quicksilver by the reins. She was nickering and trying to yank free from Blue's grip. Pooder's horse, too, was acting anxious.

"They smell water," Pooder said. And for the first time in memory, he was right about something. The horses had sensed that water was nearby. At the base of the sandstone cliffs, they discovered a trickling stream that had cut a narrow swath through the rock. There was a pool of clear water at the bottom. The boys could hardly keep up with their horses as the beasts clambered for the lead to reach the life-giving pool.

After drinking and resting in the cool shade of the overhang, Blue volunteered to climb to the top to see if the stranger was getting close. Pooder waved a hand, approving of the idea but not volunteering to go instead. Blue reached hand over hand, grasping what little handholds he could find in his quest to reach the top. Once there, he cupped a hand over his eyes and began scanning the horizon. At first, he saw only desert, empty and foreboding. There were buzzards circling lazily, probably trying to decide whether whatever poor creature they'd spotted was worth the trouble. Then, far off but coming fast, he saw what appeared to be a rider leaving behind a trail of dust. The rider seemed to be headed straight for them.

Blue yelled down to Pooder. "I think I see him, and he's still after us! We gotta get a move on!" He slipped and slid all the way to the bottom. Pooder was holding the reins to both horses by the time Blue reached the bottom. They mounted up and started out for town. It was then that Blue realized a horrible truth: They neither one knew where they were or which way Desert Belle was. They could be riding right back into a trap.

Chapter Nineteen

"What are we gonna do? We don't know where we're goin'." Blue's voice cracked with increasing panic. "That fella likely knows this land like you know the saloon. We're cooked, I'm tellin' you."

Pooder wasn't ready to share Blue's doomsday scenario. He'd had all he wanted of the gun-wielding stranger who'd threatened to do them bodily harm, and he wasn't about to give in now.

"If we can just get back to the road, we know it will lead somewhere. They don't make roads that go nowhere. We just have to stick to the road, once we find it. The first town we come to will surely have a sheriff. We'll find him and tell him our story. That owlhoot won't dare come up against the law, not after what he tried to do to us."

"I'm not so sure," Blue said. "He looked desperate, to me. Did you see those squinty eyes of his? They darned near burned a hole in your head while you were trying to get out of your drawers. Weren't you payin' attention?"

They rode in silence for some time, both unsure of their destination and growing increasingly wary of assuming that no evil deed goes unpunished. All they had on their side was one six-shooter. Blue hadn't even checked to see how many bullets were in it. He knew the thing carried six if the cylinder was fully loaded. But many gun-toters carried only five in the gun, letting the hammer rest on the empty chamber, in case they should drop it. That way it wouldn't accidentally go off and shoot their foot off, or worse. When they came to a place where the land suddenly dropped off into a gulley with steep granite sides that no horse could negotiate, Blue pulled up. He looked around, certain they were surrounded by a thousand Apache warriors, all with murder in their eyes.

"Now what? Do you see any way down besides this sheer cliff?"

"N-No, but I'm lookin'," Pooder said with a quaver in his voice. He turned his head every which way but up and finally came to an obvious conclusion: There was no way out but back the way they'd come. The look on his face was full of despair mixed with growing panic.

Blue saw it too. "There ain't no way out of here except the way we come, is there?"

Pooder sighed with unaccustomed resignation. "Nope. None I can see."

Blue looked back. "That cloud of dust is gettin' bigger. He's comin' fast, and we're about to become no more'n rabbits on a spit."

Pooder suggested they backtrack just enough to make the stranger think they'd found a way out, maybe get him to pass by without seeing them. That could give them precious time to come up with a real escape plan. They urged their horses between the thick cacti and down a slight incline. There they found enough brush for cover that they could wait for the man to pass; then they'd strike out back the way they'd come. They dismounted and hunkered down as low as possible, consider-ing they had no way to conceal their horses. And they waited. And waited.

Several minutes passed before Blue whispered, "He should have passed by now. Where do you suppose he's gotten to?"

"Probably scourin' the whole damned desert so's he don't miss us. Now I wish we'd taken his horse too."

"A body can't leave a man out here in this desert afoot. Why, that'd be considered murder, pure and simple," Blue said. Of course, this particular man had nearly plugged them. Blue was convinced that Pooder's accidental fall—causing the stranger to tumble down the hill and bust his head wide open—was all that stood between them and certain death. And now it was looking more and more like they hadn't really escaped at all, merely prolonged their agonizing wait for the bony finger of the grim reaper to reach out and send them to eternity. He'd heard tell of such at the knee of a very superstitious mother, and his Cajun father had done nothing to dispel his fears.

"Well, I'm goin' to go behind them saguaros over there to pee. Holler if he comes before I get back," Pooder said.

"So you can take off and leave me to fend for myself?"

"Blue, how can you even think such a disrespectful thing? I'm cut deep." He then took off at a lope without looking back.

"While you're out there, put your pants on the right way. You look like a fool."

Blue sat down on the gravel and began chucking rocks at a prickly pear several feet away. He tired of that soon enough and began drawing lines in the dirt with a stick off a paloverde. He waited for quite a while. Finally, exasperated, he figured Pooder had fallen into a cactus patch while trying to adjust his pants, and he figured he'd have to rescue him. He started out in the direction his friend had taken. Just then, he heard Pooder calling out to him from much farther up the trail than he expected.

"Where the devil did you get off to?" Blue called.

"Up here, up the hill. And I've got better news than a story about free food in the *Desert Belle Bugle.*"

Blue followed a narrow, winding path made

either by wildlife or trickles of water during a rain. It wandered slowly up a hill. When he came around a mesquite tree, he spotted Pooder standing out in the open where he could be seen for miles.

"Get down, you fool. He'll see you and come a'runnin'."

"He ain't goin' to see me, 'cause that cloud of dust wasn't made by his horse. It was made by the Butterfield stage comin' back to Desert Belle. That's what."

Blue ran up the hill to Pooder's side. He cupped a hand over his eyes and whistled.

"You're right. That ain't dust from the stranger. And the stage is on the road we couldn't find. All we got to do is head after it." Blue was grinning from ear to ear with this turn of fortune.

"Yeah, well, there still is the problem of no letter," Pooder said, dejected by the prospect of what could come when they faced Molly McQueen. "And we still don't know what happened to the stranger."

"You are for sure right about that. We got to put our minds to both problems."

"Time's a-wastin' Pooder. What's your plan? We can't wait no longer, and that's a fact," Blue growled, his patience clearly nearing an end.

"Okay, okay, here it is," Pooder said, all puffed up with confidence in his latest scheme.

Blue scowled and narrowed his eyes at Pooder.

"I been thinkin' hard on it." The pig farmer from Ohio took a deep breath and began laying out the most bizarre piece of pomp and circumstance heard this side of the legitimate theater.

Blue's eyes nearly popped out of his head when he heard his friend describe his grand plan. Zeb Pooder, who up to now had not been noted for his brilliant decisions, had outdone himself by concocting the most ludicrous scheme Blue had ever heard.

"Lawsy sakes, Pooder, what in tarnation makes you think Miz Molly will believe a fool thing like that?" The disbelief on Blue's face, and the shake of his head, looked to Pooder very much like criticism, which he didn't take a liking to.

"You wanted a great plan; well, this is it. And it'll work too."

"Plan? You call tellin' Miz Molly that her valuable letter got shredded by a cactus a plan?"

"Here's how it all lays out . . . one more time. We tell Molly that a terrible thing happened to her letter. When she asks what happened, you blurt out, 'Sorry, ma'am, but a powerful strong, swirling wind blew up all of a sudden. It knocked me down and grabbed the letter right outta my hand and slung it across the desert, where it ended up torn into a thousand tiny pieces on the terrible barbs of an acre of cacti. Why, we near cut our hands to pieces tryin' to retrieve all them torn-up bits. We had to finally give up or bleed to death.' "

"And what do I say when she starts to throttle me?"

"You say, 'There weren't nothin' a body could do to save that valuable paper. So I reckon you'll just have to write another, and we'll sure as shootin' get it to the stagecoach this time.' "

"You don't really think she's goin' to believe me, do you? She ain't no fool. You, on the other hand—"

"You sayin' my idea ain't sound as a dollar?"

Blue just shook his head as he stared at a mound of manure, which he quickly saw as a fair representation of what he was hearing. His forlorn look revealed his growing despair. All hope seemed to be abandoning them by the second.

"And just where do you figure on us gettin' jobs afterward?"

"What do you mean?"

"We're goin' to lose our payin' work as soon as she sees what unreliable idjits she put her faith in. Hope you still got some greenbacks tucked down in your boot, 'cause we're goin' to need to eat before long."

"Aw, she'll understand."

"She isn't going to understand anything but that we are unreliable fools who can't be trusted to do anything right."

"Okay, then you come up with a plan, Mister Know-It-All." Pooder crossed his arms and gave Blue an "I'm waiting" look.

The two mounted up and started the long trek back to the road to Desert Belle and certain doom. The whole thing would likely amount to a quick dismissal, if not worse. That was Blue's assumption, at least.

Once they had the proper direction settled in their heads, the boys struck a course that they hoped would bring them out about a mile behind the stagecoach. In minutes they came upon the dusty road and fell in where the coach had recently passed. The dust hadn't yet completely settled from its passing.

"I say we spur these cayuses to a trot so's we can catch up and maybe beg a ride into town. It'd be nice to get out of this saddle," Pooder said.

Blue nodded his agreement, and they spurred their mounts to a quicker pace. As the dust behind the coach got thicker, the boys were beginning to rue their decision to catch up to it, but, since they'd come this far, they decided to go ahead. They were nearing the rear of the coach when Blue called out, "Hold up, Pooder! *Now!*"

Pooder pulled back on the reins, and the boys stopped in the middle of the road, watching the stage as it grew more distant.

"What the devil did you do that for? We was

about to catch up. They'd surely've offered two hot, tired boys a ride if we'd asked 'em."

"Didn't you see what was tied to the luggage boot at the rear of that coach?"

"Wasn't lookin', why?"

"There was a horse tied to the backstrap. The rider must have been inside."

"So what? Lots of fellas bring their horses along when they take stage. It's so they'll have something to ride when they get to town. Nothin' special about that."

"Nothin' unless the horse belongs to somebody we ain't hankerin' to see anytime soon."

"And just who would that be, Blue?"

"The stranger who threatened to plug us if we didn't hand over the letter, that's who."

Pooder's eyes went wide with surprise. He looked at Blue and said, "Looks like we just slipped the noose once again. Somebody up there *is* lookin' after us."

Chapter Twenty

"Is he dead?"

A nod.

"What happened?"

"I hear noise and see him pull knife to kill Kelly."

"And *you* finished him off?"

"Mmm."

Kelly took that to mean yes. He stared at the body lying at his feet. Spotted Dog had replaced his own knife in the sheath in his woven belt. Joe Clutter's knife was on the ground near where Kelly had been sleeping. Kelly picked it up.

"I'd better go find the sheriff. It's his jurisdiction. You stay with the body, but don't let anyone else in here."

Again, Kelly was met with little more than a grunt, which he assumed qualified as an agreement in Apache lingo. He returned with the sheriff quickly. Hawk Burns looked as if someone was holding a gun to his head and about to pull the trigger. His face turned pasty white when he glanced down and saw Joe Clutter's corpse, its lifeless eyes wide open, as if to ask why.

Burns was muttering curses under his breath. "This ain't gonna sit well with Hank and Bob.

Those jackals are going to come after *me* for this."

"The fact that this man tried to knife me in my sleep suggest anything to you, Sheriff?"

"What do you mean?"

"Well, the Clutters obviously figure I'm a threat to them for some reason. Got any idea why that might be?"

"No. Should I?"

"Have you talked with them concerning our conversation?"

"Mighta mentioned it. What're you sayin'?"

"I told you I had seen Hank Clutter dealing off the bottom. Do you figure that knowledge could have inspired them to want me dead, rather than have to pick up and move their very lucrative crooked game to some other town?"

"I suppose it might. But I got nothing to do with it—not their gambling or the attempt on your life. My word on it."

"Uh-huh. Well, I reckon you better get the undertaker down here to haul off this trash, and while you're at it, you might stop by and tell the other Clutters they need to plan a funeral."

"Now, hold on, Marshal. I can't go in there and say somethin' like that. You killed him—it's your job to tell the next of kin. I want nothing more to do with the whole mess." The sheriff was growing more nervous by the second. His hands began a palsied shake.

They stared at each other for a short eternity. Suddenly, Hawk Burns began looking first at Kelly, then at Spotted Dog. What he observed seemed to catch in his throat. His brow furrowed with deep lines of concern. Then it hit him. Hard.

"W-Wait a minute. I don't see you carryin' a knife, Marshal, but I see the Injun's got himself a Bowie."

Kelly said nothing.

"You didn't kill Joe, did you? That heathen Apache did it. That's why you want *me* to tell the Clutters and get myself killed. Ain't that it? Why, when the town finds out one of our own was murdered by a savage, they'll come lookin' to lynch someone. I wouldn't want to be around when that happens, no sir." Burns spun like a top to flee the scene as quickly as he could.

Kelly and the Apache watched Sheriff Burns dart out of the livery, kicking up dust with every hasty step. Kelly gave the sheriff's words consideration before turning to Spotted Dog.

"He may have a point. You go to the place where we made camp along Ambush Creek. I'll meet you there as soon as I finish some business here."

"No need me to watch back?"

"I'll be all right for now. It'll take some time for the Clutters to get enough of the townsfolk heated up to consider a confrontation with a U.S. Marshal and his deputy."

"I am deputy?"

"I reckon you are now."

"I get piece of silver for shirt?"

Kelly grinned at the thought of giving Spotted Dog a badge, but the more he thought about it, the idea grew on him. Making it official would go a long way toward keeping Spotted Dog clearly on the side of the law, rather than some savage out to kill whites. He went to his saddlebags and jammed his hand under the flap. He drew out the old and somewhat tarnished badge he'd carried on his first assignment. It would do. He walked over and pinned it onto the Apache's shirt. He stood back to admire the piece of tin, then nodded in approval. Spotted Dog had a subtle grin on his face.

"Consider yourself sworn in. Better get started."

The Apache threw his blankets onto his pinto pony, swung onto its back, and made tracks for the designated rendezvous point. He knew it well. Near where the two of them had made camp the night before was the very spot where seven soldiers from Fort Huachuca had met their bloody demise nearly ten years ago, when, early one morning, they were savagely overrun by a band of renegade Mescalero Apaches who had jumped the reservation.

The Indians had intended to make it to Mexico before they were spotted and rounded up by the Army. But when they reached the creek, nearly dry at the time, they saw their only escape route blocked by soldiers. The soldiers were mostly made up of new recruits and had no knowledge of the Apaches having escaped from San Carlos. The Indians assumed the Army had indeed been warned to be on the lookout for them and were poised to attack. The band saw an attack as their only option, as to retreat meant facing an even larger contingent of soldiers at their backs, so they struck without warning just after dawn. The soldiers, unaccustomed to the tactics imposed by the fiercest fighters ever known, were quickly overcome. All but two perished in the span of thirty minutes. Thereafter, the place was known as Ambush Creek.

Marshal Kelly had every intention of confronting the Clutters. But before he did, he marched down to the telegraph office and rapped on the counter with the barrel of his rifle to get the attention of a seedy little man sleeping in a chair at the back of the room. The man, startled, jumped up, nearly stumbling over his boots, which he'd removed and laid beside his saddle.

"Uh, yessir. What can I do for you?"

"I need to get a telegram off to Sheriff Stevens in Cochise. If you'll give me a pencil and some paper, I'll write it out for you."

The man was trying to pull up a suspender that had slipped off one scrawny shoulder as he scratched through a jumble of items on his desk. Organization apparently was neither his strong suit, nor a prerequisite for employment. When he finally located the requested items, he yawned, then handed them across the counter. Kelly touched the end of the lead to his tongue and set to jotting down his message. He was particularly interested in finding out what Alex Bond looked like. As an afterthought, he figured he might as well get a complete description of the three bounty hunters too. Before handing the note to the telegrapher, he added a hello for Nettie.

"When I get an answer, where can I find you, Marshal?"

"Bring it down to the livery. If I'm not there, the owner will know how to reach me." He dropped a coin onto the desk and marched out, straight for the Shot-to-Hell Saloon. Before entering, he looked over the doors to see if the Clutters had yet arrived to set up their sleazy game of cheat'em poker. They were nowhere to be seen. He went in and approached the bar-tender, who was busy setting chairs back on the floor from atop the tables. He had a mop and a bucket nearby. The pine flooring still showed spots of moisture where the whiskey and beer-soaked surface soaked up the water more slowly.

"Mornin', Marshal. Lookin' for someone in particular?" The bartender leaned on his mop as he wiped his free hand on his apron.

"The Clutters. They been in?"

"Naw. Too early even for them. You can leave a message, though. I'll make sure they get it."

"I doubt you'll want to be the bearer of the message I intend to give them. Thanks." Kelly left the saloon just as a wagon rumbled by. It was carrying the body of Joe Clutter and was beginning to attract a few onlookers. Two or three of them fell in behind the wagon and began following it to the undertaker's place of business. They gathered around as the body was pulled from the wagon by willing hands and carried into a build-ing with several lines of gold-leaf lettering on the window. The sign proclaimed that the proprietor, besides being the town's undertaker, was also a cabinetmaker, carpenter, and painter.

Kelly watched for a couple of minutes to see the reaction of those gathered, then went back to the livery, found the owner out back currying down a bare mare with a course brush, and told him he was leaving, where he could be found, and why.

"I knowed that Joe Clutter was no good. Too consarned quiet for my taste. It's the quiet ones that you got to keep an eye on." The liveryman tapped at his temple to indicate he figured Joe Clutter might not have been of sound mind. "Don't you worry none. I won't let on where you are off to. And you can be sure when that tele-gram comes, I'll get it right out to you." He gave the marshal a wink, then went back to brushing the horse as if the whole thing was business as usual.

Kelly thanked him and saddled up the black gelding. He rode out of town to the south but doubled back once he was out of sight. He circled around to avoid running into any of the towns-folk who might report to the Clutters where he had gone and headed back north to meet the Apache. After some time, he arrived at the meeting site. He noticed Spotted Dog squatting atop an outcropping of boulders, surveying the surrounds like a sentinel. As he dismounted and let the gelding's reins drop, he walked to the place they'd camped before. Spotted Dog trotted in to meet him.

"You see anyone coming from Desert Belle?"

"No one come."

"Then we'll stay here until Mr. Banister comes out with the telegram answer. Might as well get comfortable. We could be here a while."

"Singing wire carry words quick?"

"They sure do. Sheriff Stevens already has my message, and he'll likely get back to me yet today. That is, if he's in town and awake."

"Why he sleep when sun fill sky?"

"I've known John Henry for quite a while. He's getting tired. Weary of watching his back for gunslingers and cowards and drunks. I 'spect he's startin' to think of retirement. Heaven knows, he's earned a good rest."

They built a fire and got coffee started. The nearby creek ran clear with good water. The stream came from the mountains and had a decent flow most of the year, except for a couple of months in the hottest part of the summer. Although, in southeastern Arizona Territory, it was sometimes hard to know when the hottest part was, things being somewhat subjective from one scorcher to another. Kelly was thankful that the water was, for the time being at least, cool and plentiful.

Midmorning the next day, Henry Banister rode into their camp waving a piece of paper. He got down from his horse and dropped onto the dirt near Kelly. He took off his hat and swiped an arm across his brow.

"Whew, it's bound to be a hot one, Marshal."

"Were you careful to check if you were being followed?"

"Sure did, just like you told me. There weren't nobody behind me, for sure."

"I see you have my answer."

Henry handed the envelope to the marshal. Spotted Dog handed the liveryman a cup of coffee, which the man refused, asking for some cool water instead. The Apache laid the cup aside, got an empty one, and handed it to Banister. He then pointed to the stream as if to say, "Get it yourself." Banister got up and sauntered to the stream. When he returned, Kelly had finished reading the telegram. He stuffed it into his pocket.

"You want me to send an answer?"

"Nope. It looks as though I'll be heading for Cochise, after all. I'd appreciate it if you don't confide in anyone about where you found us or where we're headed."

"My mouth's closed tighter'n a bear trap. Count on me."

"Do the Clutters know about their brother yet?" Kelly asked.

"The sheriff wasted no time lettin' word get out that Joe was the victim of a savage's knife. Since you're the only one around with an Indian ridin' with you, I 'spect they got it figured out by now." Banister mounted up and rode off toward town.

Spotted Dog looked at Kelly with an unspoken question on his face.

Kelly returned to reading the telegram. "I still don't have a description of any of the men we were following. Sheriff says he only saw Bond once, and that was from a distance too great to get an idea of his features. That means we're headed to Cochise to see what we can find out on our own."

"Me come?"

"You come. For now, you're still on the payroll, and I want you as far away as possible from the Clutters."

Chapter Twenty-one

Kelly and Spotted Dog arrived in Cochise early the next day. They went straight to the sheriff's office. Dismounting out front, Spotted Dog asked if the marshal minded that he didn't go inside. Kelly understood the bad memories the Apache might have from his previous time there. Kelly went in alone. The Apache squatted near the door in the shadow cast by the false front rising up to give the building the look of an impressive two stories, which it wasn't.

Sheriff John Henry Stevens was busy sweeping the floor near the wood-burning stove when the door opened. He brightened at the sight of the marshal.

"Piedmont, I sure am glad to see you safe and sound."

"Whatever gave you the impression I might not be?"

"Your telegram sounded somewhat ominous. Not knowin' who might be lookin' to plug you in the back. That ain't a comfort in my book."

"It's not quite that bad. Although, it might have turned out differently if Spotted Dog hadn't been lookin' out for me."

"What happened?"

"A cardsharp, one of the Clutter brothers, took issue with my mentioning to the sheriff that I saw them dealing off the bottom of the deck. He thought it might be easier to put a knife in me than to move on to a new town."

"Spotted Dog had to kill him?"

"Yep."

"I'm glad I'm just a poor ol' sheriff in a calm town," Stevens said, shaking his head. "You come back here for any particular reason, other than to see Nettie, of course?"

"You said you hadn't gotten a good look at Bond the time you saw him. That right?" Kelly said.

"Yep. Wouldn't know him if I saw him walk in right now."

"What about his clothes? Anything unusual that you remember?"

John Henry rubbed his chin as he mulled over Kelly's question. "The wind was whippin' up a storm, and he was down by the livery when I saw him come out leadin' a horse. Looked like most fellas, I reckon. Nothin' special, except . . . hmm."

"Except what?"

"Well, I do remember thinkin' first off that *you'd* snuck back into town without droppin' in to see your old friend."

"Me? Whatever gave you the idea it could have been me?"

"Why, it was them boots he was wearin'. Just like you wear. Them stovepipes."

"Sounds like that solves one part of the mystery. What can you tell me about the bounty hunters?"

"Mean-eyed, shifty, scruffy bunch. Well-worn denims and dirty shirts. One wore a cloth vest, I think. Hell, the place was so smoky, it's a miracle I remember that. Then, when they come after their guns, I was woke up so rudely from a sound sleep, I was, er, a little foggy, I reckon."

"That's all right. You told me enough."

"Say, where's that redskin?"

"He's outside. He didn't want to visit your steel-bar hotel. It seems he has some less-than-favorable remembrances of the place." Kelly laughed and turned to leave.

"I understand. Can't say as I blame him. Where you headed now? As if I didn't know."

Kelly stood in the doorway staring across the street at Nettie's restaurant. Spotted Dog stood up. Their eyes met, and Kelly knew instantly that the Apache was thinking the very same thing he was. "I like your idea, my Chiricahua friend. Let's get a bite to eat."

The sheriff grabbed Kelly's sleeve. "Hold on. I ain't so sure the townsfolk are goin' to take kindly to sharing their meal with an Indian. How about I get some food brought over here?"

Kelly's face turned dark. He fought to maintain

his calm demeanor. He'd had enough bigotry to last him a lifetime. But Stevens' words weren't meant to insult. They were meant to spare the Apache any embarrassment that might come from some customer's rude remarks or actions. He looked at Spotted Dog.

The Indian understood. He nodded. "That good idea."

Kelly removed his cavalry-style Stetson and scratched his head. "All right. But I'll go over and have Nettie fix some vittles for you two. I'll bring them back soon as they're ready."

Both the Apache and the sheriff nodded their approval of the idea. The marshal hurried across the street to beat a buggy being driven by a man in an obvious hurry to get someplace. He removed his Stetson as he pushed open the door. Nettie was just serving a couple when she heard the bell tinkle and looked up to see him smiling at her. Her face lit up. She excused herself and came to him, taking his arm and directing him to a table away from others.

"It is *so* good to have you back," she said, barely above a whisper. She gave him an enthusiastic hug.

Keeping his voice down also, he told her about Spotted Dog, the concerns he and the sheriff had about bringing an Apache into the restaurant, and asked that she come up with some dinner for the two of them. He said he'd take it over to the jail and come back afterward so they could spend some time talking alone. She bristled at the thought that any of her customers might not accept the Indian, but she acquiesced nevertheless. After all, it hadn't been that long ago that Spotted Dog helped save her life at the hands of a deranged murderer.

Nettie brought out two trays brimming with steaming food, and Kelly headed across to the jail. After he'd attended to the dining needs of the sheriff and the Apache, he and Nettie were finally able to sit and talk. She asked if he'd found the men he was following.

"It's beginning to look as if those bounty hunters attacked Bond at his ranch. It also looks like he got the best of them. He may have buried them under a pile of rocks he blew out of the side of a canyon not too far from Ambush Creek. From there, it appears he went on to Desert Belle, although I have no idea why."

"Maybe he figured the sheriff would come lookin' for answers if the bounty hunters never came back for a reward. Didn't you say the bounty hunters thought he was a fugitive from New Mexico?"

"That's a possibility, for sure. But all along, John Henry felt they had the wrong man."

"Why would they attack him, then? When they saw him, wouldn't they know he wasn't the man they were after and ride on?"

"You'd think so. But bounty hunters are a strange lot, and thinkin' straight ain't always their way of doin' business."

"It's hard to imagine one man taking down three gunmen."

"Yes, it is. And that's why Spotted Dog and I are going back out to the Bond spread to have a closer look around."

"When are you leaving? Can you wait and go tomorrow morning?"

"I'll have to find a place to put the Indian up for the night. Maybe the—"

"He can stay right here in the back room, and I'll entertain no arguments. No one goes in there but me. We can fix him a comfortable place to sleep with some blankets on the floor. It's quiet back there."

Kelly thought about her proposal, knowing that Spotted Dog would not look favorably on any suggestion by Stevens that he sleep in a jail cell, and finally saw it as a reasonable solution. He accepted, saying he'd go get the Indian and be back soon. When he left, Nettie began washing the dishes, sweeping the floor, and putting things away in preparation for the next morning's breakfast customers. By the time Kelly returned by the rear entrance, the place was cleaned and ready for business. When they came in the door, Nettie smiled at the Apache and motioned for him to follow her. Spotted Dog at first looked apprehensive, but as soon as Nettie pointed out that there was coffee on the stove and that he could drink as much as he wished, his grin gave him away. The plan would work. Piedmont and Nettie saw no need to lock the door behind them as they left.

The next morning, Kelly and Spotted Dog were on their way out to the Bond ranch bright and early. Kelly had no idea what he'd find there, but he had to have a look. Nothing was adding up as to how three men might have ended up dead, while a fourth man lit a shuck for Desert Belle. Or so it appeared. But why?

When they arrived at the Bond ranch, Kelly asked Spotted Dog to look around outside for anything that might tell them exactly what had happened when the bounty hunters came to call. The place was quiet, with no sign of there ever having been wranglers employed, at least not in recent times. The barn was empty. Dust lay thick on everything. It had become a ghost ranch. But that wasn't only because the owner was gone. There was no sign of there having been any activity for months, perhaps years. The corral, barn, and outbuildings had fallen into disrepair from neglect and harsh weather. Winds roaring down from the mountains from fast-moving thunderstorms had torn shingles from the barn, and no one had bothered to replace them. Incoming rain had soaked what little hay was still in the barn loft, causing it to rot and become moldy.

Kelly went through the house, passing from room to room, perusing anything and everything that might answer the question: *Who is Alex Bond?* In the bedroom, he found clothing hung neatly on pegs along the wall and a pair of stove-pipe boots standing straight as soldiers on the floor. Oddly, a pair of worn cowboy boots had been tossed in a corner, along with a dirty shirt and vest. A dresser, its drawers filled with shirts and socks folded in an orderly fashion, sat next to the bed. *The man certainly is particular about his belongings,* Kelly mused.

In the main room, a fireplace made of stones rounded from years of rushing water from the nearby river that dropped from the mountains to the north took up nearly one whole wall. The wooden floor was clean and showed no signs that it had welcomed spur-dragging cowpokes with no regard for the finer things in life. No, Alex Bond was clearly a man who liked order. He lived it, demanded it of himself. There was no sign of a woman or children ever having lived in the house. Much of the furniture looked new, likely ordered from eastern mail-order houses. Bond was living the life of a wealthy gentleman, not a struggling rancher. But where did his money come from? What business was he in, if not cattle or sheep? His ranch wasn't large enough to support the herd of longhorns it would take to afford Bond's apparent lifestyle. And where the house was situated, boxed in by rocky hills and steep cliffs, there was no access to open range.

Kelly sauntered into Bond's office, where a large walnut desk with polished brass drawer pulls and a top inlaid with fine leather took up considerable space. He'd had only a brief chance to look over Bond's papers when he was here with Sheriff Stevens. Now he planned to take his time and give the place a more thorough going over. He started with a leather-bound ledger that he found in the top middle drawer. The rows of numbers lined up perfectly, one above the other, and showed a person of exacting penmanship. Two pages had been torn from it. Bond appeared to have rather sizable holdings all over southeastern Arizona Territory. From Desert Belle to Charleston, and from Cochise to Tombstone. He seemed to control a diverse business portfolio. The ledger indicated he owned at least a substantial part of three mines, two hotels, and half a dozen saloons, all of which were quite profitable. But, while there was plenty of evidence of keen business acumen, not one iota of evidence surfaced to indicate that he was, or had any connection to, Alex Bowdre. None.

Clearly, the bounty hunters were on the wrong trail. But who put them on that trail in the first place, and why did their arrival end in blood-shed? From Sheriff Stevens' description of Bond as a man who wore stovepipe boots, and finding a pair of the same style in the bedroom, all the evidence pointed to Bond doing in his pursuers and then carting their bodies off for an unceremonious burial under a dynamite-induced landslide. But why did Bond then continue on toward Desert Belle? Why not haul the corpses into Cochise and turn them over to the sheriff? Could it have had anything to do with the mention Kelly had seen in one of the letters among Bond's papers alluding to financial problems at the Gilded Lily Mine? The correspondence was from an Abner Dillard. Kelly shook his head as the questions mounted, and the answers eluded him. He gathered up a number of letters that were scattered about, along with some personal business papers, and stuffed them into his saddlebags. He would look them over later on his trip back to Desert Belle.

While his arrival in Desert Belle likely wouldn't be met with open arms, it was an unavoidable trip. And, although the reason for Spotted Dog's help in tracking the bounty hunters was at an end, he figured Spotted Dog and his Spencer might still come in handy—especially since he figured the Clutters might be looking to even the score.

Chapter Twenty-two

"What're we gonna do now?" Pooder asked.

"We sure can't be seen in town, so I reckon the only thing left for us is to follow the road until we can take the cutoff to the Lily. Might as well face our punishment, gather up our belongin's, and strike out for the first town that'll have us."

Pooder shrugged. "Yeah, might as well take our medicine. Get it over with. But I sure ain't lookin' forward to the tongue-lashin' we're gonna get from Miz Molly. I'd almost rather swig a whole bottle of caster oil."

Blue shivered at the thought. When he was much younger, before his mother had died of a fever, castor oil was an ever-present threat when he'd been tempted to stretch the boundaries of her patience—something young boys seemed unable to avoid. The memory of that foul-tasting potion rose in his throat with the suddenness of a flushed covey of quail. He swallowed hard to send it back into the dark cavern from whence it came.

"Could we ponder on something more pleasurable than—"

"Hmm. Why, sure, Blue. Sorry to discomfort

you. You must have the same distaste for that thick brown goo that I always figured would be best for lubricatin' wagon wheels but not desirable when forced on you by a ma with fire in her eyes."

Blue didn't respond to Pooder's reminiscing about his family conflicts. He stared at a spider that had sprung from a hole under some brush mashed down by passing horses or cattle. Pooder looked perplexed, seeing that he seemed to have lost Blue's attention.

"Hey, what's got you so tied up in knots? You ain't worried about what Miz Molly's gonna do to us when we get back, are you?"

"Some, I reckon, but that ain't all."

"Yeah? What're you talkin' about?"

"I been wonderin' how that fella knew we had that letter and why he wanted it so bad."

"Probably figured it had money in it or something. Ain't hard to figure why a fella like that would do almost anything for money. Those Clutters ain't shy about wantin' *my* money, are they?"

"How did he know we would be comin' down that dusty old Tucson road when we did? And you ain't come up with how he knew we had somethin' he wanted," said Blue, scratching his head and screwing his mouth into a puzzled look.

"Just give me a minute to puzzle it out. Can't be too difficult," Pooder said, scratching at a mosquito bite on his arm that had become a red welt. "Maybe he overheard you and me talkin' about it in town."

Blue silently questioned the possibility of that happening, and he had to admit, neither of them had made any great attempt to keep it a secret. And Blue had gone to the stage office, himself, asking about getting an important letter onto the stage. Or had he? Now he wasn't certain what had transpired during his quest to make sure Molly's letter got delivered.

"I, uh, suppose it's possible. But I ain't givin' up on the idea that he found out some other way."

"What other way?"

"I don't know. I just feel like there's somethin' real wrong about the whole situation, and we're right in the middle of it. I can't figure why a fella would want to kill us for a letter. It just don't make sense. We need to talk to someone who might have the answers."

"Who might that be, Blue?"

"The onliest one who knows what was in that letter: Miz Molly."

Pooder frowned at the suggestion that he might have to face Miz Molly sooner rather than later, which would have been his preference. But he knew Blue was right. Unless they knew why the letter was important, they'd never know why someone had tried to kill them for it. He figured he'd go along with his friend, at least for now.

"Okay, Blue, we'll head for the Lily and let the chips fall where they may."

They cut cross-country in the general direction of the mine. Pooder figured it to be about an hour's ride. When, after two hours, they hadn't crossed the mine road, Blue was making noises that suggested Pooder couldn't find his own butt. Another hour found them coming through the far gate, waving to the fence rider and slowly making their nervous way to the cluster of buildings that constituted the center of the mine's operations. When they drew up in front of Molly McQueen's office and began to dismount, the boss lady had already spied them and was standing on the porch, hands on hips and scowling something ferocious. Blue knew they were in for a serious tongue-lashing at the very least. He had no idea what the very worst could be.

"Uh, howdy, Miz Molly, er, boss. We were—"

"Get your lazy behinds down off them horses, you two no-accounts, and get inside. I don't want to shoot you out here in the open where a witness might turn up unexpectedly." She turned and stormed into her office and, holding the door open, tapped her foot impatiently.

"Yes, ma'am," muttered Blue, as he dismounted gingerly, not quite certain whether she was joking or not. He'd never seen her this mad before, and he didn't like the tone of her voice.

When they entered, she ordered them to sit

down. "Now, which one of you fools is going to start making an accounting of your past two days? And just where is my letter? Did it get onto the damned stage or not? I want answers, and I want them now!" She slammed her hand down on her desk so hard that a large book that had been placed precariously close to the edge fell off, crashing to the floor with what sounded like a gunshot. Blue jumped, his eyes wide with fear. Pooder started sweating profusely and wriggling in his chair. He suddenly had a serious urge to visit the outhouse.

Molly looked from one to the other. "Well?"

Pooder opened his mouth to speak, but Molly put a hand up. "Not you. Blue, you tell me what happened, and don't leave anything out. Not one thing—do you understand?"

"Yes, ma'am," Blue said, his voice just above a whisper. His mouth was so dry, he thought his lips might stick together as he tried forming words. He sighed with resignation, then took a deep breath and began from where he'd found the letter in the dirt where Pooder had dropped it in his haste to get to the gambling table. Pooder turned red at the telling, embarrassed by how stupid his actions were sounding and what Miz Molly must think of him.

Blue went on to explain about Quicksilver breaking a shoe and the man who stopped to help. And about how when he got to town, the stage was already gone. Then he went on about finding Pooder hiding behind some crates in an alley, and about them deciding the only thing to do was to ride to Tucson to deliver the letter themselves. All the while Molly's expression transformed from mere curiosity to staring bullets at Pooder for his lack of responsibility.

"I can see that you were faced with a tough decision, but you haven't told me what happened to the letter."

"Yes, ma'am, I was about to get to that. Uh, well, it—"

"What Blue's tryin to say, boss, is that there was this huge storm that come up and near blew us into the next county, and gusts—"

"Shut up, Pooder. I know when you're about to start blowin' smoke into my face. Go ahead, Blue. You're the only one here who'll tell it straight."

Blue launched into their heading for Tucson, then deciding they could turn off at the road to Tombstone and put the letter onto the train in Contention City. When he got to the part about the stranger demanding they give him the letter, Molly's face turned dour. Clearly, she was trying to piece something together that wasn't making sense. Blue had to back up and tell her about the real storm and how they almost lost the horses. When he told about being dragged through the dirt and gravel by Quicksilver, she winced at the damage being pulled over cacti and sharp rocks could do. She put a hand to her mouth and clucked her tongue.

"It wasn't so awful, ma'am. I didn't get no broken bones or nothin'."

"Hmm. I'd say you're lucky. So, when the man told you to hand over the letter, what did you do?"

"Well, he was wavin' that gun—er, *this* gun—in our faces," he said, pointing to the Remington stuck in his belt, "and I figured you wouldn't want anybody to get killed over a letter, so I reached into my shirt pocket to give it to him."

"So, what did he do when you handed it to him?"

"That's just it, ma'am," Pooder blurted out. "We didn't give it to him, 'cause it had got tore out of Blue's pocket after the storm and all that draggin' and such."

"Where did the letter get to?"

Both boys hung their heads, and Blue muttered, "We don't know. It's lost."

Molly couldn't make up her mind whether to laugh or cry. On one hand, without the letter getting to Mr. Alex Bond, their deal was off, and she would be faced with shutting down the mine. On the other hand, the way the boys had tried to persevere in the face of such overwhelming odds was heartening, even if Pooder *was* still the darnedest fool she'd ever known.

She said nothing for several minutes as she

mulled over the situation. Then a thought came to her. She got up, went around her desk, and began shuffling through several stacks of papers. She finally came to one that caught her attention, folded it, and screwed up her face in a very serious frown.

"You boys get the wagon hitched up and bring it around front. We're goin' to town."

"Does that mean we ain't bein' kicked off our jobs?" Pooder said with a hopeful smile.

Blue jabbed him in the ribs with an elbow. Pooder let out a squeal, rubbing the place where Blue had gotten him, expecting a bruise.

Molly gave them both a squinty-eyed glare. "If I can't make sense of all this, there ain't *one* of us goin' to have jobs after today. Now, get that wagon ready."

As Blue and Pooder rushed out to do Molly's bidding, Blue said, "You know, I can't make heads or tails out of this here letter. How come Miz Molly didn't tell us what was in it? And she didn't jump all over us near as bad as I figured she would."

"Yeah, I wondered the same thing. But we better get the wagon hooked up, or I can see things goin' sour real quick."

Pooder went to the barn to tug out the wagon while Blue went to the corral to cut out a pair of Belgians to pull it. Molly had chosen several Belgian horses to pull wagons back and forth to town because they were powerful and not nearly as stubborn as mules. Blue led his two favorites through the corral gate and to the barn. Pooder was ready with the wagon. It would take only a few minutes to get the horses hitched up and ready.

Molly was stomping across the yard just as they finished. "You boys get aboard. Blue, you drive," Molly growled, and she climbed onto the steel step and launched herself onto the seat, handing the reins to Blue, who smiled broadly at the trust she'd placed in him.

No one said a word for the first half hour. Blue was perfectly happy to wait and see where they were going and what they'd do when they got there. Not so with Pooder. The impatient, nosy pig farmer was always ready with questions. This time was no exception.

"Miz Molly, you got any idea why that fella was fixin' to kill us for that letter?"

All he got in the way of an answer was a blistering frown from Molly McQueen.

Chapter Twenty-three

As the stage rumbled into Desert Belle, it skidded to a stop in a cloud of dust in front of the hotel, and the tall stranger in stovepipe boots and a brown felt hat stepped out. He looked up at the driver, thanked him for the lift, and proceeded to untie his horse from the luggage boot. He led his mount to a watering trough, let her drink her fill, and then continued down the street to stop in front of the gunsmith's shop. He tied the horse to the rail and went inside. A bell tinkled as he opened the door. A smallish man, with thinning hair and a hawklike nose, was working intently at a polishing machine at the rear of the shop. In his hand was a nickel-plated frame for a Colt revolver. He looked up at the sound.

"Howdy, stranger. Hot enough out there for you? Anything in particular you might be lookin' for?"

"I find I'm in need of a hogleg. I favor a Remington. You got one that you guarantee will shoot fast and straight? A used one would do. I ain't all that particular about how it looks," the man said. His expression suggested he brooked no nonsense, especially where his shooting iron was concerned.

"Cain't guarantee either one. All depends on who's holdin' the piece. Got some nice Remingtons, though. A couple of them were traded for newer. Step on down to the end of the counter." The man reached in, pulled out a . 45-caliber Remington that looked as if it had been well used, and laid it on the counter. "What become of the one you had? I see you got an empty holster."

The man didn't say anything. He picked up the revolver, cocked it, dry-fired it to test the trigger pull, slipped it into his empty holster, and said, "Decent balance. How much, old man?"

"That one'll cost you twenty dollars."

"Toss in a box of shells, and you've got a deal."

The gunsmith mulled that over for a minute, then said, "Fair 'nough." He reached around behind him and took a box of cartridges from the shelf.

The stranger reached into his pants pocket and pulled out some greenbacks. He counted out twenty singles, then put the remaining bills back into his pocket. He nodded his thanks and wandered out the door.

He walked slowly along the boardwalk, stopping to glance in at each business and shop, until he came to the Shot-to-Hell Saloon, whereupon he pushed through the swinging doors. Standing just inside, he looked the place over for a minute, then sauntered up to the bar. The bartender wasted no time asking what he'd like. The shot glass of amber whiskey had no sooner been poured than the bartender said, "That was a good thing you done yesterday, gettin' poor ol' Abner free of the clutches of them card mechanics, friend. Reckon he ain't eager to return, though. I ain't seen him today."

"You seen a couple of young boys around here? Seventeen, eighteen? One is a skinny black boy; the other looks like he ain't good for nothin' but honey dippin'."

"Don't know any black boys, but the other sounds like Zeb Pooder. He comes in most every Friday. But, nope, I ain't seen him in here today. I figure Pooder ain't any more eager to come back and get himself scalped by them Clutters than Abner is. Why is it you're lookin' for 'em?"

The stranger stared at him with cold eyes, then turned away without answering. He gazed across the room, probably looking for familiar faces, like two scared boys who might have slipped in unnoticed by the bartender. Seeing that they weren't there, he quickly downed the whiskey and walked outside. The bartender shrugged at the slight and continued to wipe down the oak bar top.

The stranger seethed at losing those two rapscallions *and* his Remington. The only thing that had gone his way was, in their haste to escape his clutches, the boys had left his horse behind; for if they hadn't, he'd still be out there in the sun, without water or shelter and, by now, probably dead of heatstroke. He had no idea whether they'd left his horse out of pity or from sheer forgetfulness. Either way, he was here now and alive and darned eager to get revenge. As well as get his hands on a certain letter.

Since Desert Belle had acquired two more saloons during the past year, they were close by and easily visible, one from the other. That way it was easier for drunks to stumble from one to the next with less chance they might sober up sufficiently to change their minds and ride on back to their own bunkhouse. The stranger wandered into the next saloon, and the next. He found no sign of the two boys who had snatched victory from him by getting away with the letter he wished to obtain. He stopped under the balcony in front of the hotel, leaned against the wall to roll a smoke, and puzzled over what his next move should be.

He had half of what he'd come for, but he wanted it all. And it was within reach. But what chance was he taking, hanging around town? If he pulled off his scheme, he'd be rolling in money. If he slipped up, he could be dangling from the end of a rope. He'd seen the sheriff and sized him up as nothing to worry about. If the lawman hadn't had the nerve to call out such blatant card cheats as the Clutters, he sure wasn't about to brace a man who had the look of a professional gunslinger. He was just about dead certain of that. Maybe he'd just wait around long enough for those two boys to show up. They were his ticket to complete success. If they didn't appear in town in a day or two, he could always take the money he had and ride on, with no one the wiser. Unless, of course, someone stumbled onto the "package" he'd left in the desert no more than a half mile from town. He wasn't really worried, though, because buzzards and coyotes made short work of corpses, especially skinny ones.

The stranger went back up to his own hotel room. He turned the key in the lock and pushed open the door, stopping briefly to look down the hallway both ways to be sure no one was watching. Then he slipped in and locked the door from the inside. He took off his hat, tossed it onto the floor by the metal-frame bed, and dragged the only chair in the room over to the window. He'd asked for this particular room for a couple of reasons: First, it was next to Abner's room, and second, it gave him a view of the main street and anyone who might be coming into town from the direction of the Lily mine.

Smoking wasn't permitted in the hotel rooms because the town council had deemed the risk too great for a fire. It wouldn't take much to start a conflagration that could level an entire block of all-wood buildings. He drew a package of papers from his pocket and shook some tobacco out to make a cigarette, ignoring rules for which he had no use. He struck a Lucifer on the windowsill and lit up. He muttered something to himself about doing what ever he darned well pleased, and the town council could take a roll in manure for all he cared. He opened the window and pulled back one side of the lace curtain to get a perfect view down the street. He sat and smoked and grinned at his great fortune. He looked over at the bed, whereupon lay a leather satchel with the initials *AD* emblazoned on the flap.

He could hear the people on the street below, talking, laughing, and discussing the heat or the price of beef or a new strike nearby. Then he heard boots in the hallway. He pulled his Remington and turned toward the door. But the footsteps faded down the hall, and he relaxed, shoving the revolver back into its holster. *Must be getting a little jumpy,* he thought. *Get control of yourself.*

He heard the rattle of wagons, none, however, coming from the direction of the Lily. As he waited and watched, his tension grew. Mulling over his various options, he grew increasingly nervous, lighting one smoke after another. He looked around several times as if the leather satchel on his bed might get up and sneak out of the room on its own.

Where are those damned kids? When I get my hands on that letter, this whole town will have to sit up and take notice of me.

He thought about what he'd do when he had his deal all sewn up, when he was part owner of the Gilded Lily. Maybe he should just settle down here. It didn't seem like a bad place to settle. No one knew him, and the sheriff wouldn't be any problem. In fact, he was surprised that a growing town would even put up with a do-nothing sheriff like Hawk Burns, a man who seemed to have the spine of a rope. Yes, he was feeling pretty good about everything—everything except that all-important letter that would give him the security he'd sought all his life.

He got to his feet and went to the satchel to once again marvel at its contents. He'd never seen so much money before, at least not in his possession. He pulled a fistful of it out and spread it like a hand of cards. He dropped it back into the satchel and gave out a hooray, as if he'd just struck a vein of gold. And, once he had the letter in his possession, he figured it'd be just like drawing to an inside straight and clearing the table.

He began to think it was time to celebrate at the Shot-to-Hell Saloon. Maybe he'd treat himself to a bottle of brandy—the good stuff, not that watered-down whiskey they usually served —and maybe spend a little time with that real pretty gal who was singing when he was there last. He went to the washbowl and poured some water into it from the pitcher. He splashed water on his face, then wet his hair to get it to behave more civilly. He ran a comb through it and, satisfied with what he saw in the Chatham mirror, left his room, being certain to lock it behind him. After all, if anyone knew how much money was stashed under his bed, that flimsy lock would prove an inadequate deterrent to thieves. The thought made him chuckle as he went down to the lobby, taking the stairs two at a time.

Fifty thousand dollars, he thought. *Whooee!*

Chapter Twenty-four

Hank and Bob Clutter had spent most of the day and part of the early evening tossing back shot after shot of rotgut whiskey and managing to get drunker by the minute. None of the other patrons of the Shot-to-Hall Saloon dared even approach them with the suggestion of a game of poker. For the regulars—those who'd seen pot after pot end up in the clutches of these unpredictable gamblers—caution won out. For those wise in the ways of mean, drunken gamblers, none gave any consideration at all to even engaging the two Clutters in conversation, let alone suggesting a game of chance, for fear of doing or saying something to set off an instantaneous and potentially deadly response from the volatile brothers. And right now, the two appeared ready to explode.

"What're we gonna do about that marshal and his murderin' savage?" Bob growled.

"We're gonna get our revenge, that's what. You don't think I'm goin' to let a thing like the cold-blooded killin' of our brother go unanswered, do you?"

"So, how do we go about it? It ain't easy to kill a marshal and get away with it."

"I'm figurin' on that very thing right now."

"Poor ol' Joe's body ain't hardly cold, and that marshal's out there somewhere, free as a bird. It ain't right, I tell you. It just ain't," Bob said, slurring his words and gazing at his brother through half-open, bloodshot eyes.

"First off, we're goin' up to the Dunham place and get her to tell us where we can find that skunk of a lawman. She knows him. I heard her say so. Probably knows where he is. Then we'll get some shut-eye—make our plan in the mornin'." Hank pushed back his chair, nearly dumping it over backward when one of the legs got hung up in a splintered gap between planks where some cowboy had gotten liquored up and shot a hole in the floor. He caught himself before falling on his backside, straightened up, and wobbled for the door, with Bob, equally inebriated, right behind.

They staggered into the street and turned uphill to find Mrs. Dunham. When they reached the two-story, clapboard-sided house—one that had recently been painted, shutters repaired, and with flower beds in bloom and carefully weeded—they stumbled up the steps. Hank pounded on the door.

Mrs. Dunham yanked the door open and stood there wiping her hands on her apron and scowling. "What do you mean pounding on my door like two savages that ain't been housebroke?

What's the matter with you two drunken fools?"

Hank had nearly fallen over a wicker chair as she surprised him by pulling open the door and shouting at him before he could even think what he was there for.

"We, uh, we're here lookin' for that marshal. Him and that savage killed our brother Joe. And we intend to make him pay for it. Now, where is he? We know you're a f-friend of his." He tried to jam a finger into her face to make sure she understood he was serious, but she apparently had seen enough tough drunks in her time to know what to do. She slammed the door in his face so hard, the glass rattled. Her reaction surprised him so much, he fell backward down the steps and ended up sprawled in the dirt on his back. Bob stumbled off the porch after him, missed the second step, and ended up facedown in a cloud of dust next to his brother.

Pushing himself up onto one knee, Bob mumbled, "Don't seem like we're goin' to get much outta the old biddy. Let's go get us a drink."

Hank groaned. "Too many drinks is why we're lyin' in the dirt, dummy. We need some coffee." Bob helped Hank to his feet, and together they staggered back down the street to a nearby restaurant. The smell of freshly brewed coffee wafted through the door as they went inside and fell into the first two unoccupied chairs they came to.

After the coffee came and the restaurant owner had gone back to serving serious customers, Hank leaned on the table for support and stared at the checkerboard pattern in the tablecloth. Bob splashed hot coffee down the front of his shirt before finally taking a drink. They sat without either one saying a word for several minutes, hoping they could clear their minds sufficiently to come up with a rational plan for getting even with the marshal. An hour passed, and after the restaurant owner had refreshed their coffee cups several times, Hank finally began to speak without slurring his words.

"That damned lawman let an Injun murder our little brother, and we got to make him pay. Can't let this go. You know that, don't you?"

"I know it. But I still ain't sure what Joe was doin' at the livery with a knife. You got any idea?"

"I, uh, reckon I sorta, uh, suggested that we'd be better off if that marshal, uh, well if something were to happen to him. . . ."

"You told him that? You know Joe does whatever you say. *You* got him killed!"

"I didn't *make* him go. I just suggested that it would be good if—"

"Yeah, I know—if that marshal accidentally fell on a knife. That was *your* knife Joe was carrying, wasn't it?"

"Mighta been." Hank hung his head. Bob was staring a hole through his brother with enough anger in his eyes to start a fire in damp wood.

"What do we do now? I say we pull up stakes and head for Charleston," Bob said. "No use hangin' around here any longer. That marshal is sure to figure we'll be gunnin' for him. He's likely to shoot us on sight. You thought any on that?"

Hank was still slumped in his chair when the restaurant owner sauntered over and asked if they'd like anything else. He said he was eager to close up. Hank started to argue with the man, but Bob stopped him and took him by the arm, pulling him out of his chair. Dropping a couple of coins onto the table, they headed for the door. They stepped outside just as the sun was beginning to set. They both stopped at a bench on the boardwalk and plopped down. Hank was shaking his head and muttering something about life not being fair as Bob pulled out a plug of tobacco and bit off a chunk. A lady leading a young boy walked by, giving Bob a sour look as he began chewing the tobacco. *Yes, lady, I know it's nasty, but it's my damned business,* he thought as he scowled back at her. Then he spat in the dirt. She stuck her nose into the air and hurried along.

The air was still heavy from the day's heat, and the smell of horses, lathered up from their trip in from mining camps and ranches within a ten-mile radius of the town, filled his nostrils with an unpleasant smell. A smell he was sick of. Truth be known, Bob Clutter would just as soon be farther north—Montana, maybe, or Wyoming, where there was grass and trees and clean air, and a man didn't feel sweaty all the time. He had never told Hank how he felt, because he knew it was futile to suggest such a move to his stubborn older brother. Desert Belle had been Hank's choice of a good town to make a killing in with his crooked deck. Things hadn't exactly worked out the way Hank had expected, but he wasn't about to admit it was time to cash it in and try another town.

They sat on the rickety bench without speaking for the better part of an hour, as the town fell into darkness and the saloons came alive with noisy drinkers and gamblers flush with Friday's pay and ready to throw their money away. Bob had an itch to get back to the tables so he could fleece some of those eager young marks. Hank, on the other hand, was deep in thought, still bent on revenge, unable to accept his part in his brother's death. That's when the idea came to him. He pushed himself up and took a couple of steps out into the street.

"Where you goin'?" Bob asked.

"I'm goin' to find out where that marshal is hidin'."

"Hidin'? What makes you think he's hidin'?"

"You don't see him and that savage struttin' up

and down the streets, do you? He knows we're gunnin' for him, and he's too big a coward to stand up and face us. So, we'll just go to him."

Bob scratched his head. "I ain't so sure that marshal is scared of us. He didn't look to me like the kind who'd scare easy."

"Take my word for it. I know the type. He'll back down plenty fast when we brace him. And when we're through with that badge-toter, we'll finish off that savage."

"Where do you figure to start lookin' for them?" Bob was frowning with doubt as to his brother's evaluation of the marshal's cowardice. But he'd never really been strong enough in his own beliefs to challenge Hank. This time was no different.

"They were staying down at the livery, weren't they? That's where we'll start. I'll lay odds that old man Banister knows exactly where to find them two. And if he gets forgetful, we'll help him remember." Hank slammed a fist into his other hand to make his point.

Hank's rekindled interest in getting back at the marshal for Joe's death was making Bob very nervous.

"C'mon, brother, quit hangin' back. The sooner we find out where they are, the sooner we cancel the debt on Joe." Hank grabbed Bob's sleeve and tugged at him as if he was a reluctant child.

When they got to the livery, Banister was

pitchforking manure into a wheelbarrow. He looked up as Hank and Bob came toward him. Hank strode right up to the man and thrust out a hand, grabbing Banister by the collar.

"Wh-What's goin' on here, fellas?" Banister said, choking from Hank's tight grip.

"Where's that marshal and his stinkin' Injun?"

"H-How should I know? You don't see them here, do you?"

"I know they told you where they could be found when they got that telegram. The telegraph operator is a friend of mine, and he told me. So, no more of your dumb act. Tell me right now, or so help me—"

"Hold on, Hank. If Banister says he don't know nothin', I believe him. No reason to get all riled up."

"Shut up, Bob. I know what I'm doin' here. Now, Banister, I'll ask just one more time. Where are they?"

Banister was trying to claw Hank's hands loose from his collar, but the bigger man was too powerful. He was being lifted off his feet. He still had the pitchfork in his hand, and he tried to bring it up to where he could jab Hank and make him let go. Hank was instantly incensed at Banister's bold struggle to get free. Rage was building in him like a boiler about to explode. Bob could see Hank's face turn beet red, his teeth making a grinding sound.

"I-I tell you, I don't kn—"

Hank's free hand slipped down to his six-gun. He yanked it from its holster, cocked it in one smooth motion, and jammed the barrel into Banister's stomach. "Last chance, old man!" he growled.

"A-Ambush Creek."

Hank pulled the trigger anyway and let go of the liveryman. Banister dropped to the ground. A pool of blood gathered around his limp body. Banister didn't move. He was dead before he hit the dirt.

"What'd you do that for? He told you, didn't he? Now you've done it, you damned fool. I always knew that temper of yours would get us hanged." Bob's face was pale at the sight of the scrawny old man lying at his feet, dead eyes staring at the roof.

"Just you shut up! I need time to think!" roared Hank.

"You better start thinkin' of a way out of here before the sheriff gets wind of this."

"Saddle up. We're headin' for Ambush Creek."

Chapter Twenty-five

After riding nearly the whole day, Piedmont Kelly and Spotted Dog were approaching Ambush Creek and the spot where they'd camped before.

"We'll stop here for the night. I'd rather ride into Desert Belle in the daylight. No tellin' where the Clutters might be hangin' back in the shadows, waitin' for us to wander into their sights."

Spotted Dog grunted his approval of the plan. "I find food. Meet you at same place." The Apache dug his heels into the pony's ribs and rode off toward the same low hills where he'd found plenty of plump rabbits for the taking when they'd last camped by the water.

Kelly hobbled his black gelding so he'd be free to drink from the stream or munch the occasional patch of tough grass. Then he started a fire and set up camp. At Spotted Dog's mention of food, Kelly's stomach began to growl, yearning for Nettie's home cooking. Just the thought of her gave him a warm glow. He shook it off, knowing he'd get back to Cochise soon—right after he cleared up the mystery of Alex Bond.

There was something uncomfortable about

camping where so many soldiers had lost their lives. He felt a sudden melancholy sweep over him, as if the place hadn't seen its last shedding of blood.

When the Indian returned, the fire was ready, and he set to skinning the two rabbits without delay. Both men were hungry and tired. They made quick work of their food and two cups of coffee each. As Kelly leaned back against his saddle, he noticed Spotted Dog, illuminated by the flickering flames of the dying fire, polishing his new badge with a shirtsleeve. He turned away and smiled. He remembered when he'd first pinned on a tin star as a deputy sheriff back in the town in which he grew up, the town where his minister father was gunned down by outlaws. He still carried with him the pride he had felt at being acknowledged as responsible enough to earn the town council's trust. When he turned back to say something to the Apache, Spotted Dog was slumped over, sound asleep.

About a half hour before dawn, Kelly was awakened by a strange sound. Something barely audible, but also unexpected. And not an animal. He slowly opened his eyes without moving his head. A shadow fell across his face. There was someone in camp. He couldn't see the Apache, but something told him it wasn't the Indian stirring about. He slowly and carefully eased his hand out from under his blanket, reaching as quietly as possible for his revolver, which he kept next to him. His fingers touched the holster, but he was instantly aware that his Colt was no longer in it. Just then a familiar voice spoke up.

"Don't bother lookin' for your piece, Marshal. It ain't there," Hank Clutter said, contempt in his voice and Kelly's Colt stuck in his belt. "Climb on outta them blankets and face your last moments on earth like a man. I don't fancy killin' a man in his bed."

Bob stepped closer and gave Kelly a kick in the stomach.

"Best you do what my brother says, else I'll just have to stomp you good," Bob said, a cold bitterness in his voice. Having the upper hand had lessened his apprehension at bracing a marshal. He felt himself getting braver by the minute. "You shouldn't have let that Injun kill our brother."

"Come to think of it, where *is* that savage?" Hank hissed.

Kelly eased the blanket off and got to his knees. His Winchester was still lying just under the edge of the blanket, out of sight of the Clutters, with a cartridge already chambered. He always slept with the carbine lying parallel to his leg so he could get to it quickly. But under the circumstances, he wasn't certain he could get them both before he took a bullet himself. He snuck a quick glance over to where Spotted Dog had been when he went to sleep, but there was no sign of the Apache now. In fact, there was no sign he'd ever been in camp. *Curious,* he thought.

"I have no idea what you're talking about," Kelly said with an innocent shrug.

"I reckon you know, but it don't make no difference. We got you," Bob growled.

The Clutters had spaced themselves far enough apart, and several feet away, that he knew his options were limited. If he dove for the rifle, he might get off one shot, but he couldn't be certain he would even hit anything in such haste. He was, however, certain one of the Clutters would easily get him, unless they were such bad shots that they couldn't hit a barn twenty feet away, the likelihood of which he had his doubts. Few people in their profession—that of running a crooked gambling game—could have lived as long as they had, had they been terrible marksmen. At this point, about all he could do was hope that the equation might somehow change in his favor.

Just as he was considering what might accomplish that, his prayers were answered by a voice filled with the obvious desire to not let the Clutters leave the camp alive.

"You ready to die?" Spotted Dog stepped from behind a boulder, his Spencer rifle aimed directly at Hank Clutter.

The two men studied each other for a moment. Hank knew he wouldn't live to draw another ace from his sleeve if the Indian fired, but Bob might easily then get the Apache, and since the marshal didn't have his revolver, he, too, should be an easy mark. None of them knew what was going through the Chiricahua's mind at that moment, but Kelly saw the situation as getting tenser by the second.

"How'd you find me, Hank?" the marshal said.

"It took a little convincin', but old man Banister spilled the beans," Hank said with a snicker.

Bob reacted to that comment sharply. "Yeah, but you still had to blast a hole through him, didn't you, brother?" The anger in his voice was difficult to understand. Here he was, apparently ready to gun down the marshal, yet he objected to his brother's killing the liveryman.

"Shut up, Bob."

"Why? There ain't nothin' he can do about it now."

"Bob's right, Hank. You got the upper hand here. Go ahead and tell me what happened. Can't make any difference, can it?" Kelly said.

Hank seemed confused by the way the conversation was going, and he was getting increasingly nervous. His eye twitched, and he chewed his lip.

"Both of you, just shut up!" Hank raised his revolver toward Kelly. Bob was looking at his brother when Spotted Dog's Spencer erupted in a smoky blast that hit Hank in the chest, knocking him to the ground. Bob's eyes grew wide. He seemed too shaken to move. That was all the time Kelly needed to dive for his Winchester, pull back the hammer, and aim it at the last remaining Clutter.

Bob froze. Spotted Dog chambered a new cartridge and brought the Spencer up. His intent was clear. He had no compunction to talk. He was ready to act.

Kelly held up a hand. "Hold off, Spotted Dog. Let's see what this hombre's intentions are."

The Indian stayed at the ready but held back.

"What *are* your intentions, Bob? Shall we end this here and now, or are you coming back to Desert Belle with us peaceable like?"

Bob Clutter was about to make the most important decision of his life. If he went with the marshal, he might escape the rope, but not a stint in prison for plotting murder. He hadn't been the one to pull the trigger on Banister, and Hank had all but admitted that in front of the marshal. He'd cheated lots of folks out of their hard-earned money, but murder? No, never. Then again, would anyone believe him? Was it better to just end it all right here? As he stared blankly, seeming to be considering his options, Marshal Kelly took two rapid steps forward and made his decision for him. Kelly grabbed the revolver out of his hand and threw it into the dirt. Bob hung his head in defeat.

The Apache lowered his rifle. "What we do with him?" he asked.

"We'll think of something. Let's saddle up and head for Desert Belle."

Chester Banks, a traveling salesman for the Great Western Miners Supply Company out of St. Louis, was on his way down to the livery to rent a buckboard. He'd come in on the Butterfield stage the day before, the one that had stopped to pick up an extra passenger in the desert. He knew every one of the several mines in the area to call on that might be needing to buy replacement parts for machinery, or an assortment of pulleys, sets of block-and-tackle, cable wire, and specialized parts for stamping machines. He carried catalogues and some small free samples with him to leave behind as an incentive to order from his company. With the rented buckboard, he could cover about three mines a day. He figured a week total and he'd be back on the stage for Bisbee, a hotbed of copper mining.

When he strode into the livery, the place was quiet with the exception of the buzzing of flies, which seemed particularly plentiful so early in the morning. But then, there was no place more abundantly supplied with manure, either, and flies went with the territory.

"Hello, Mr. Banister. It's Chester Banks," he called out from the front entrance.

He waited a couple of minutes before calling again. He got no answer. He decided Banister must be out back, so he leaned against the door frame and pulled out a cigarillo. He pulled a Lucifer from a tin box in his coat pocket and struck it against the rough wood. He lit his smoke and tossed the match into the dirt outside to avoid a possible fire. He drew in the smoke and let it out in rhythmic puffs, trying to create smoke rings. As he waited for Banister to come back up front, he was puzzled at not hearing anything. *Maybe he's taking a snooze,* he thought. *Maybe I'd better go back and see where he is.* He wandered back toward the tack room. He passed several stalls before coming to where Banister repaired harnesses and saddles. That's when he saw what was attracting all the flies.

He jumped back at seeing the old man lying on the floor in a pool of blood. At first Banks thought the man had fallen and possibly stuck himself on the tines of a pitchfork or something. Then the obviousness of a bullet wound quickly made itself abundantly clear. He ran from the livery straight for the sheriff's office, yelling all the way. Sheriff Burns stepped out at hearing the commotion. Chester Banks' hollering had attracted the attention of a number of citizens, who quickly began gathering in front of the jail.

"What's all the fuss about?" Hawk Burns demanded. He stood in the doorway, hands on his hips, looking with displeasure at whoever was disturbing the peace.

"Sheriff, my name is Banks, and I just came from the livery, where I had intended to rent a buckboard from the owner. But when I got there, I found the poor man lying on the floor, dead as a stump. Looks as if he'd been shot."

"You say Banister is dead?" A murmur rose from those who had gathered with Banks.

"Most assuredly, sir. Quite dead. Come see for yourself," Banks said, and he turned on his heel to lead the crowd back to the livery. Hawk Burns followed with a frown furrowing his forehead. He spat a stream of tobacco juice into the dirt, strolling along as if he was simply part of some local parade. It wouldn't have surprised anyone if he'd chosen to wave as he passed the several onlookers, like a king to his subjects.

When they arrived at the livery, two or three people pushed by Banks to be the first to see what the ruckus was all about. The first one to come upon Banister's body let out a gasp. Some turned away, others strode quickly back outside, having seen all they intended of the murdered man. Hawk Burns asked if anyone knew if there had been any animosity shown toward Banister, and, if so, who was most likely to be angry enough to kill him. No one knew anything. The sheriff sent for the undertaker, shooed everyone outside, and told them to go on about their business. He said he'd handle things and that they shouldn't worry. He was in charge.

As the crowd slowly dispersed, several muttered about there being no chance in hell that Hawk Burns would find an answer to who the killer might be. Most shook their heads in disgust, and some even suggested it might be time for a new election, a year early.

Sheriff Hawk Burns spat some more tobacco juice and grumbled about a man not being allowed to get a nap for all the nonsense going on in town.

He didn't wait for the undertaker.

Chapter Twenty-six

As the wagon rattled along, Molly was scouring the desert for any sign of Abner Dillard returning to say the deal had been made. She saw nothing, not even a sleek coyote making its way stealthily through the underbrush in search of a quail. Blue had the reins, and Pooder sat in back, whistling and trying to fashion a hangman's noose out of a short piece of rope he'd found in the bed of the Studebaker. Molly was grim, her frown so intense, she looked as though she were staring through narrow slits cut in her face. Clearly she didn't want to talk; her jaw was clenched tightly, and Blue wasn't about to test her by trying to engage her in idle conversation. But he did wonder what thoughts were going through her mind. She certainly wasn't happy about the tight spot he and Pooder had put her in. He fully understood that. Although he wasn't entirely clear on what it was *he* could have done differently, especially since he couldn't have foreseen Quicksilver breaking a shoe and nearly leaving him stranded in the desert. And losing the letter to a storm and a startled horse, well, how could he have prevented any of that? After all, he had tried his best to get the letter to Tucson, although he had no idea what was in it or why it was so important.

It had been Pooder's complete lack of responsibility that started things going downhill, without any doubt, but even then, Miz Molly had had no guarantee of things going perfectly smoothly. Why, all sorts of things could have gone wrong. In defense of his friend, Blue began silently rationalizing the many possibilities, many of them so farfetched, even with his vivid imagination, he almost laughed out loud at some of them. Laughing at a time like this would be met with disdain, so he wisely kept his thoughts to himself, contained within a somber expression.

Quite suddenly, Molly pointed to several buzzards circling ahead. They seemed to be lazily marking a place about fifty yards off the road, a half mile ahead. She clucked her tongue.

"Reckon we're not the only ones around bein' visited with a passel of bad luck. Looks like some poor critter has breathed his last."

Pooder looked up from attempting to hang his own wrist to gaze off at what Molly was talking about. He wiped the sweat from his brow and squeezed his eyes to get them to focus. He looked, then looked again. He finally stood on tiptoe, bracing himself with a firm grip on the back of the driver's seat. He cupped one hand over his eyes for shade, shaking his head.

"I-I don't think it's a critter, Miss Molly. I think it might be a man."

"Wh-What! A man, you say?"

"Yes, ma'am. I can make out what looks like a white shirt and some red suspenders."

"Red . . . ! Blue, make for them buzzards. And as we get closer, take a couple of potshots with that six-gun you got tucked in your belt to scare 'em off."

Blue did as he was told, whipping the horses to a run and turning the wagon off the road and out into the desert. The wheels crushed cactus plants and sank into the sand every once in a while, but he kept the reins firm, occasionally slapping the animals on the rump so they wouldn't be tempted to slow down and get stuck. He managed to pull the Remington and fire a couple of wild shots into the air. It worked, and the buzzards backed off their quarry as the wagon rumbled to a dusty, sliding stop. Molly was climbing down off the seat almost before Blue had secured the reins around the brake handle. She started screaming as she lifted her skirts and stumbled toward the bloody, almost indistinguishable creature that lay ahead.

Molly reached the body first and fell to her knees, crying and shaking her head.

"No! No, no, no!" she cried. She bent over the corpse of Abner Dillard, a pitiful sight already ravaged by creatures of the desert.

Blue and Pooder stood behind Molly, eyes wide and trembling with fear.

"Abner, Abner, what happened to you? Did you try to walk back to the Lily and collapse from thirst? Tell me you didn't do something so foolish—"

Pooder took that as the time to make an observation. "Looks to me like he was shot, Miz Molly. There, that big hole in his shirt, see? I'd say that's what done him in," he said, puffing up a bit from his keen observation.

What he got back from Molly was a sharp glare, her face pinched like a prune. He gave a guilty twist of his mouth and looked away. Molly turned back to Abner's body, shaking her head and moaning.

Blue figured it was time to take a position about their next move. He wasn't interested in standing in the heat without a hat any longer, staring at a ripped and torn decomposing body.

"Ma'am, what do you think we should do?" he proffered. "We should have a plan."

She stopped rocking and seemed to take his comment under advisement. She sighed, wiped a tear away, and said, "You're right, Blue. We have to do something. I suppose we ought to take the poor soul into town and let the sheriff handle the situation. And I reckon I'm forced to agree with Pooder. It looks like someone done him in."

"Yes, ma'am," Blue agreed, but he didn't really

favor picking up a dead body and spending the next two hours with it bouncing around in the back of the wagon. He was wise enough to recognize, however, that his choice in the matter wasn't likely to be negotiable.

"Pooder, you take his feet, and I'll take his arms. We'll carry him to the wagon and slide him onto the bed. Blue, see if you can get the wagon any closer. I don't want to have to carry him any farther than I have to."

Blue jumped at the chance to avoid any physical contact with the dead. He'd surely already had enough of that in his young life. He hurried to the Studebaker and scrambled up into the driver's seat. He slapped the reins, and the horses grudgingly obeyed the command to move forward. They were skittish, sensing something disagreeable in the vicinity. The closer they got to the body, the less willing they were to pull, shying and trying to yank the reins out of the boy's hands. But Blue didn't yield to their head shaking. His insistent snapping of the reins provided sufficient incentive, and the horses drew the wagon up the slight hill to bring it alongside where Abner lay.

"Good, Blue. Now, Pooder, grab hold, and we'll heave him up into the bed."

With a grimace, Pooder obeyed. Getting it over with as quickly as possible seemed the best course of action. The two of them lifted Abner into the wagon, and, unconsciously wiping her hands on her skirt, Molly climbed up beside Blue, leaving Pooder to remain in back with Abner's body, a situation he found most disagreeable. However, he was wise enough to know that this wasn't the time to bellyache, so he stood close to the front, clinging tightly to the back of the seat, preparing himself for a torturous ride into Desert Belle.

As the wagon rumbled into town, Molly told Blue to keep going and pull up in front of the sheriff's office. "Don't stop for nothin' or no one," she admonished.

Blue snapped the reins and let out a whistle that pricked the horses' ears, and they obeyed with a lunge. When he yanked back on the reins and stomped the brake in front of the jail, Molly called out to the sheriff.

"Hawk Burns, you no-account badge-toter, get your lazy, worthless behind outta that chair and come out here!" she shouted. Several people on the street heard her yelling as she stood up in the seat. Sheriff Burns opened the door gingerly, not knowing what to expect. Looking around, he stepped outside.

"Why, Molly McQueen, what are you screeching about? Hit a bump in the road, did you? Shake your bustle loose?" The sheriff grinned as he stepped into the street.

Molly said nothing. She just pointed to the back of the wagon, then eased herself off to the ground. Burns walked around to the back. When he saw Abner's grisly corpse, he grabbed at his stomach and turned away.

"What th—! Who is it?"

"It's Abner Dillard, my bookkeeper—or what's left of him, anyway. He was murdered!"

"Now, how do you know a thing like that?"

"Well, he sure as hell didn't wander out into the desert and plug himself, then throw the gun away. So, what're *you* goin' to do about it?" Molly was seething as she confronted a man she thought of as useless, an opportunist with no idea of what was expected of a real lawman. He was weak, and everyone knew it. She had always figured he was put into office for that very reason by the council, a council more interested in keeping the flow of money coming to the merchants than keeping a tight rein on the misdeeds of drunks and rowdies, who were often the town's main source of revenue, as well as a thorn in the side of the God-fearing folk.

Hawk Burns stroked his stubbly chin as he pondered his next move. To be truthful, he wasn't sure what to do. One of the passersby, who stopped to stare at the corpse for a brief moment, swallowed hard and tried to walk away. But Burns saw that as an opportunity to clear the street in front of his office and maybe get him off the hook. At least for the time being.

"Jeb, go down and get the undertaker. Tell him to bring his cart so he can haul this away." He turned to Molly as the man hurried down the dusty street. "Maybe he can tell us something useful. I'll let you know as soon as I hear something. You go on about your business." Deciding to waste no more time on this troublesome woman, he went inside and slammed the door behind him.

"He wasn't no help at all, was he, Miz Molly?" Pooder blurted out.

Molly was spitting mad. She could hardly keep her composure. Yet she didn't know where else to turn for help. Where had the marshal gone? He would find the scoundrel who'd perpetrated this despicable act on sweet old Abner. She struggled to hold back more tears.

"You reckon we ought to get the wagon out of the street and go back to the mine, Miz Molly?" Blue said. She was startled at his suggestion that they leave town before Abner's murderer was brought to justice. She couldn't just up and leave. *Sheriff Worthless won't lift a finger. It's up to me and the boys to figure this out. And I aim to do just that.*

"Blue, soon as the undertaker gets here, you take the wagon to the livery. Pooder and I'll get us rooms at the hotel. We're stayin' the night."

"Yes, ma'am," Blue said, hauling hard on the

reins to coax the team to turn around to make loading into the undertaker's cart easier.

From his second-floor window of the hotel, the stranger watched the scene as it played out right across the street from him. He began tapping his foot nervously. *I didn't expect the old man would be found so soon. Damn! And right there with the corpse are those two rotten scoundrels that tried to do me in. This puts me in a ticklish situation, but I'm going to have to chance it. They must have that letter—the answer to all my problems—and I aim to get it. No matter what. And who is that feisty old woman?*

He watched as Molly and Pooder headed for the hotel—and right into his hands. He couldn't believe his good fortune. *Hmm. This may be easier than I thought.*

Chapter Twenty-seven

Marshal Kelly and Spotted Dog rode into Desert Belle leading Bob Clutter, his hands tied in front of him, and Hank Clutter, his body wrapped in his own blanket and tied across his saddle. They headed straight for the sheriff's office. Kelly was not expecting a warm reception. People on the boardwalks stopped to stare. Bob Clutter looked about nervously as all eyes seemed to be on him and his dead brother.

Bob's anger at letting his brother talk him into trying to dry-gulch the marshal and the Indian showed on his face. His lips curled, his jaw clenched, and his brow was harshly lined. About the only thing he had to be happy about was that he was still alive. And, from his expression, it would have been hard to tell whether he saw any advantage to that. He certainly didn't favor having to face the future without either of his brothers. The more he thought about his sad state of affairs, the more he slumped in his saddle.

They tied up out front of the Desert Belle jail. Kelly looked around for any sign of an unfriendly reception. Seeing none, he left Spotted Dog with the horses and went inside.

Hawk Burns was sitting at his desk, a small pocketknife clutched in his bony hand, carving on a hunk of wood. Kelly thought it resembled a crude depiction of a horse. The sheriff looked up, and, when he saw the marshal, his expression turned sour.

"What do *you* want? Come back to cause more trouble?"

"In a manner of speaking, I reckon you could say that. I have a corpse and a prisoner for you to take charge of."

"The hell you say. Who did you and your savage kill this time?" Hawk jumped up as if his britches were aflame.

"Hank and Bob Clutter tried to ambush us as we slept. Seems it was in retribution for Joe's failure at the same thing. Hank had the misfortune to make a bad choice. Bob was smart enough to make the right choice. But I think a nice, long stay in your jail is warranted."

"It might be more than a stay. Some fella found Mr. Banister's body down at the livery. He'd been shot to death. A witness said he saw Hank and Bob Clutter ride away from the livery right after the time Banister was most likely killed, sometime late evening yesterday. No one heard the shot, though, mostly because of all the racket from the saloons. Damned shame. Banister was a good man."

"The Clutters admitted they'd done something

to convince him to talk. They forced him to reveal where I was camped. He was the only one in town who knew. Bob said as much when he and Hank were arguing just before Hank made his fatal mistake. They must have headed straight for our camp after shooting him," Kelly said.

"Ever since you two rode into town, I've got dead men poppin' up all over. Three, now, countin' Hank. Can't wait for you to get out of town so things can get back to normal," Burns said, shaking his head.

"Are you sayin' there's been another killing besides Banister?"

"Yep. That Abner Dillard fella that works out at the Gilded Lily Mine. Molly McQueen and them two boys that work for her found him near eaten up by scavengers somewhere in the desert between town and the mine. He'd been gunned down too. Awfulest thing you ever did see."

"When did this happen?"

"You mean, when did he get shot, or when did they find him?"

"I'm not particular. Tell me everything you can."

Burns tried to relate the story to the best of his recollection, which at times was sketchy, mostly because he wasn't fully awake when the group had rumbled into town. Molly had told the sheriff she hadn't seen Dillard since he left the Lily two days earlier. Burns, a man who spent his time in his office either sleeping or carving on sticks, hadn't seen the man before he was brought in stretched out on the bed of Molly's wagon. And he had no idea who might have wanted him dead. But then, any in-depth knowledge of most of the goings-on in Desert Belle eluded the sheriff.

But Burns' telling of the story was beginning to make some sense to Piedmont Kelly, almost as if it were a giant puzzle, although, as yet, he wasn't able to connect every last one of the pieces. His attention strayed from Burns' blathering as he remembered that some of the papers he had taken from Alex Bond's house mentioned Abner Dillard's name several times. Maybe it was time he looked at them more closely, and he could easily do that since he had brought them along, stuffed into his saddlebags.

"You said Molly McQueen and her boys brought in Dillard's body? Did she leave town or—"

"Naw. She stomped out of here threatenin' to tear the town apart until she found whoever killed the old man. I think she headed for the hotel."

"Sheriff, if you'll take charge of the corpse and the prisoner, I'll set to figurin' this whole mess out. After that, you can get back to your whittlin'." Kelly turned on his heel and headed out the door before he could see the incensed look that came over Burns at the subtle suggestion that he wasn't doing a proper job as sheriff.

When he stepped outside, he motioned for

Spotted Dog to follow him up the street toward the Dunham house.

"Bring the horses. The sheriff can handle the Clutters from here on."

"Where we go?"

"I need some time to sort this whole thing out. Mrs. Dunham's boarding house might be just the place to do it. She's got the room for me to spread out the papers I found at Bond's place. I think the answers we're seeking are in there, someplace."

Spotted Dog got that funny look on his face when he wasn't certain just how welcome he'd be in a white man's abode. Kelly noticed the Apache's puzzled expression and allowed a wry grin to curl his lips.

"Don't worry none—she won't bite."

Spotted Dog grunted at how perceptive the marshal seemed always to be.

Mrs. Dunham was sitting on the front porch peeling apples. The peels dropped into her lap, which was covered with a towel. She looked up at their arrival and smiled. That wide, welcoming smile was one of the things Kelly remembered from his first visit to town—a time that had too few good memories. But he did remember how she'd mothered him as he convalesced after being shot in the back on his way out to the Gilded Lily. And how she'd patched up the hole in his shirt almost good as new.

"Good day to ya, Marshal, and to your friend also. Have ya decided to stay after all?"

Spotted Dog remained by the horses as the marshal climbed the steps to the porch. The Apache sought to be as inconspicuous as possible. As he watched the woman, it struck him as odd that she would cut away the most colorful part of the fruit, which he assumed would then be discarded. He'd only tasted the colorful fruit a few times, and his mouth was watering at the thought. But he was certain that the hide was as important to the taste as the inside.

"I seem to remember you having a large dining room table. I need to spread out a passel of papers so I can try to unravel a mystery. I was wonderin' if you'd be so kind as to allow me a couple of hours to pore over the contents of these papers. I promise not to overstay my welcome, if you'd oblige."

"Marshal, you're more than welcome to do whatever needs doin'. Ain't got any boarders right at the moment, so I got no need to use the table—unless, of course, you two want some dinner. I was just fixin' to bake an apple pie. Don't suppose you'd be interested in a piece of that, would you?" A wry, knowing smile crossed her lips.

"Thank you, ma'am. I doubt you could keep us away once the smells of baking catch up to us. And dinner sounds fine."

Kelly went to the dining room to spread out Bond's papers. He immediately set to poring over page after page, shaking his head at each new revelation. He spent nearly two hours without saying anything. Mrs. Dunham had brought coffee, and the marshal occasionally took a sip. The Apache gulped his, once it was cool enough not to scorch his throat. He found squatting on the floor with his back against the wall preferable to sitting in a stiff, squeaky ladderback chair, which, he assumed by the sound of it, had little useful life left in it.

Occasionally, Kelly would rub his chin and murmur something unintelligible. He shared none of his supposed revelations with the Apache, however. When Mrs. Dunham came into the room, she cast a disbelieving eye at how the marshal had managed to completely fill every inch of usable space. She put her hands on her hips, clucked her tongue, and turned back to the kitchen. She called back through the door, "Marshal, I'll have something for you boys to eat in fifteen minutes. No need to gather up your work, though, because I can just as easily set a table in the kitchen. I'll holler when it's ready."

Kelly muttered something that sounded vaguely like *thank you*. Spotted Dog wasn't even certain it was a language. He returned to consuming more coffee. Suddenly, he got up and rushed outside. When he returned several minutes later, Kelly looked up and said, "I could have told you that drinking too much coffee increases the need to relieve oneself."

The Indian grinned and returned to his coffee cup.

When Mrs. Dunham called them to join her in the kitchen, Spotted Dog wore an apprehensive look. He was uncomfortable eating at the white man's table. Kelly construed the Apache's reluctance to sit down as a time to make other arrangements. He took the Indian aside and asked if he would rather eat on the porch. The Indian's eyes lit up with relief that the marshal, again, had accurately read his mind. Kelly explained to Mrs. Dunham that it wasn't anything she'd done, but that Spotted Dog had been raised to eat more primitively, and that was what he was used to. Kelly asked her if she'd mind giving him a plateful of steak, some biscuits, and beans that he could take outside and eat on the porch. He said he wouldn't mind going outside himself, since it was such a fine day. Mrs. Dunham picked up on his meaning instantly and said that that arrangement was fine with her. She made up three plates and carried them outside, handing one to each of the men, then sitting herself down on the edge of the low porch.

"I think you're right about the weather, Marshal. Makes eatin' a real pleasure when you can see God's hand in it more clearly."

Spotted Dog dug into his food with the fervor of a starving man, which, after the several fat rabbits he'd bagged over the last few days, didn't seem likely.

After dinner, Kelly returned to his careful perusal of the papers scattered about the dining room. Suddenly, as if a bright light had burst through a window, the marshal slapped the table. Spotted Dog was startled by the marshal's outburst.

"That's it! I finally figured out what's goin' on around here. And I know who our killer is. Now the whole thing makes sense," Kelly said. He looked pleased with his discovery, as he began gathering up all the papers and putting them neatly into his saddlebags. "I'm afraid it's going to come as a shock to Molly McQueen, however. We're dealing with a very evil man. And it's time we put an end to his conniving."

"We go now?" Spotted Dog asked.

"I don't look forward to it, but I reckon we might as well get to it."

"You boys in too big a hurry for a piece of fresh apple pie?" Mrs. Dunham said, holding two plates up.

Spotted Dog didn't wait for Kelly to answer.

"Not in hurry," he said, reaching for one of the plates.

Kelly just rolled his eyes as Mrs. Dunham broke out into a hearty laugh.

Chapter Twenty-eight

Molly and Pooder stood at the reception desk of the hotel. She was showing just how impatient she was to get Abner's murder solved by tapping her foot and looking around anxiously. She was more than eager to get answers as to why her bookkeeper had been in the desert alone in the first place, and who would have reason to kill him. She tapped the bell a couple of times, and when no one came through the curtains that separated the lobby from the office, she tapped it again, a little harder this time. Still no response. She slammed her hand down hard on the counter and yelled.

"Where in tarnation is everybody? You want customers or not?" Her gruff voice could be heard all the way out in the street.

Just then the curtains parted, and a fat, balding man with sweat pouring down his high forehead emerged and stomped up to the counter. He was pulling up his suspenders. His shirttail stuck out, and a couple of buttons were undone.

"Hold your britches," he said without looking up. Then, upon seeing it was a woman, he muttered apologetically, "Uh, oh, sorry, Molly, didn't know it was you. I was, uh, out back, uh, tendin' to . . . oh, never mind. What can I do for you?"

"Need a couple of rooms for a night or two, George. Put me in one and my two boys in the other. Make the bill out to the Gilded Lily. It's business."

"All right, Molly. Just sign the register, and I'll get you the keys. You can have the two rooms on the east side if you want. Already got a gent in the front, and that Dillard fella from out your way across the hall. Although I ain't seen him for a while."

"And you won't, either, unless you go to his funeral," Molly said.

"Funeral? Wh-What happened?"

"He met up with foul play in the form of a bullet."

"Mercy, what's become of the law around here?"

"Not much, I'd have to say, considerin' who our sheriff is."

"Uh, yeah, well, you still want them rooms?"

"We do." She scratched her name into the large book that lay on the counter. With the keys in hand, she motioned for Pooder to follow her. She looked back at George when she reached the steps. "When Blue LeBeau gets here, tell him where we are. You can't miss him."

"Uh, yes, ma'am," George said, wondering what Molly meant by that last remark.

The stranger had watched as Molly and Pooder
entered the hotel, and now he listened at his door
as his prey climbed the stairs. He heard them
unlock the doors to their respective rooms. He
overheard Molly as she told Pooder to keep a
watch out for Blue and to tell her when he
arrived. She said they needed to talk about
Abner's death and compare notes on who might
have done the killing. She wanted to learn
everything she could about the man who had
tried to steal the letter from them. She intended
to gather every scrap of evidence possible
before going to the marshal.

The stranger could barely contain his excitement as he saw his chance to get the boys alone,
extract the letter, and then ride out and confront
the mine manager with his proof of ownership.
Once he had possession, let them prove he'd
had anything to do with the old man's death. He
wished them luck. He had been very careful
about not leaving anything behind that could tie
him to the corpse in the desert.

As soon as he heard both doors close, he
slipped out of his room and crept along the hall.
He stopped at one of the two rooms he was
certain they were occupying. He listened with
one ear pressed tightly to the door. He heard
nothing from the room he figured that rapscallion
Pooder was in, and he assumed the boy had gone

downstairs to wait on his friend. That was all well and good. He wanted them both together, anyway. He moved to the next room. He overheard the woman humming to herself. He knocked lightly at her door.

"Is that you, boys?" she called out. She turned the knob and eased the door ajar.

When he heard the knob turn, he shoved hard against the door, slamming it against Molly and knocking her backward. She tripped over her own feet and fell onto the bed. As she struggled to recover her footing, his gun was out and pointed at her before she could utter a sound. He held a finger up to his lips to indicate she was to remain silent as he closed the door behind him. Looking down the barrel of the Remington was all she needed to convince her he meant business.

"Don't make a sound, lady, or this thing goes off. And you go to Heaven today."

"Wh-Who are y-you, and what do you w-want?" Fear rose in her like a volcano about to erupt. She was defenseless, and it was easy to see he knew it. He had the upper hand.

"I want that letter those two boys cheated me out of. Before this day is over, one way or another, that mine will be making me money, and a goodly amount, too, if I know mining. Now, where are they?"

Molly figured by the way he was talking, he didn't know who she was, or he'd be trying to make her write a new letter. At gunpoint. Then he'd have to kill her too.

"Why, they went to, uh, talk to the marshal."

"You work out at the Gilded Lily?"

"In a manner of speaking, I reckon you could say that. I, uh, am the cook."

"But you know the manager, right?"

"Oh, sure, quite well. Why, is it important?"

"If I can't wring that letter out of those two bumbling fools, you are goin' to send a message out to the mine manager tellin' him to write a new one."

"What letter is that you're, uh, talking about?"

"Never you mind. Now you just sit tight while I tie you up. Then I'll go look for them two. And if you know what's good for you, you'll stay put and not try kickin' the walls or door to attract attention. Otherwise, you'll get the same thing I gave that Abner Dillard fella. Understand?"

With a stricken look on her face, Molly nodded her understanding. She put up no fight as he tied her hands behind her and stuffed a handkerchief into her mouth. He pushed her onto the bed and let himself out, locking the door behind him.

Pooder had been restless, and rather than stay put in a small room with nothing to do except look out the window, he went down the back stairs and down the alley to the livery. He figured Blue would still be there unhitching the team.

Once they put their heads together, he was certain they could come up with a way to keep Molly from losing the mine—as long as they could stay clear of that highway robber. He ran down the alley, dodging crates and barrels that had been discarded out the backs of stores along the way. He stopped once to pick up something shiny, which he thought could have been a coin someone had dropped. It turned out to be the half-buried top of a tin can, and in his haste to pick it up, he cut himself on the sharp, jagged edge. He threw it down in disgust and continued on his way, sucking on his bleeding finger.

When he got to the livery, there was no sign of Blue or the wagon. *Must still be waiting for the undertaker,* he thought. *I'll just hang around here.* He found a comfortable bale of straw to sit on. As he waited, his wandering gaze caught sight of a dark reddish stain on the ground. *Wonder what that could be.* But soon his thoughts turned to how much money it took to own a livery, what with all those harnesses and saddles and wagons and horses for rent.

The stranger walked the boardwalk slowly, hoping to catch a glimpse of the boys. He tipped his hat to one young lady but otherwise paid little attention to others. As he was passing one of the saloons, he heard a wagon coming from the direction of the jail. Had not Blue called to the horses to move faster, the stranger might not have looked up. But he recognized Blue's voice. He smiled at his good fortune and hastened his pace to keep up with the wagon.

When Blue got to the livery, he drove the horses around to the rear, where the corral was. If the liveryman wasn't around, he'd have to unhitch the team—a task he didn't relish. Although the Belgians were gentle enough, they were big and tended to be balky on occasion.

Pooder heard the wagon rattle around to the back. He hopped off the straw and ran to the big double doors at the end of the long hallway. When Blue saw him, he figured he might at least get a little help. Not much, but a little.

"They come to haul off the dead body?"

"Yeah, it was some scarecrow in a black suit lookin' like he wasn't that far from the grave, himself. Made a chill run up my spine. You seen Mr. Banister?"

"Nope. He's probably out getting some vittles or maybe havin' himself a whiskey."

"Then it looks like the unhitchin' is up to us."

Pooder groaned at the thought of physical exertion, but Blue handed him the reins without waiting for an answer.

As Pooder was about to put a hackamore on one horse and lead her back to the corral, the stranger stepped through the door with a gun in his hand, and it was pointed directly at Pooder.

"Well, boys, we meet again. Looks like it's my lucky day."

The boys stared wide-eyed at the .45 pointed at them.

"Yessiree. I figure to get my Remington back, make you hand over that letter, and be well on the way to becomin' a wealthy man all in the course of the next half hour. What do you say to that?"

"You're welcome to your gun, mister, but as for the letter, like I said before, we ain't got it. The blamed thing got lost in the desert, and it's still out there somewhere," Blue said, hands on hips, defiant. The fire in his eyes burned with exasperation at this hombre's threats to his well-being.

The man stared back at Blue with as much determination to have his way as Blue had demonstrated against him. It was clear there was no middle ground. He had two choices: He could either kill these two or go back and get the mining camp's cook and make her send a note to the manager. He was weighing those choices when the decision was made for him in the form of a voice at the entrance yelling for someone to come unhitch his team and curry and feed them.

The stranger pushed the boys into a back stall, grabbed a length of rope, and began securing them to a post. He muffled any sound they might make by stuffing some dirty cloths into their mouths. He then scampered up front to inform the customer that there was no one around but to leave his team and buggy and it would all be taken care of as he'd requested. After several minutes of deliberations—along with considerable hemming and hawing on the part of a rancher reluctant to just turn his team over to a man he didn't know—the customer walked away, apparently satisfied.

But in his haste to tie the boys to the post, the stranger hadn't counted on Blue's ability to slip one thin arm around far enough to get to his pants pocket and pull out his jackknife. He sawed at the ropes with the sharp blade and freed them both within a couple of seconds. The ropes had no more than dropped to the floor than the boys were racing out the back door and were halfway to the hotel before the stranger returned.

When he saw that his captives had flown the coop, he was furious. He stomped out of the livery and headed for the hotel, fire in his eyes, his hand on his Remington.

"Someone's goin' to pay for this outrage!" he shouted to anyone who would listen.

Chapter Twenty-nine

When Kelly and Spotted Dog reached the top of the stairs, a faint moaning came from one of the rooms. Stopping at each door to listen, he finally came to number three. He tried the knob, but it was locked. He knocked but heard only several muffled grunts. Stepping back, he braced himself against the far wall and gave the door a hard kick. It gave way with little effort, the flimsy lock breaking easily as the door slammed against the inner wall. There on the bed was Molly McQueen, bound and gagged, squirming and fighting to get free of her bonds. A kerchief had been shoved into her mouth, making it impossible to scream for help. Her face was red with rage as she tried to spit out the gag. When the marshal came through the door, the look of relief that washed across her face was plain. He rushed to her and pulled the gag from her mouth.

"Thank heavens you two are here, Marshal," she sputtered. "That man plans to kill the boys, just like he done to poor Abner."

"What man? What's he look like? Where is he?"

"I never saw him before. Tall, thin, wearin' boots like you got on—tall ones."

"He tell you his name?"

"Not so's I can recollect."

Kelly untied Molly and helped her to her feet.

"Did he take the boys?"

"I don't know. I assume Pooder is in his room. Blue hasn't come back yet from taking the wagon down to the livery."

"So, for all you know, the boys might still be safe."

"I hope so. There's no tellin' whether Pooder will blab about where Blue got off to, if that man gets his hands on him. That boy's not bright, you know."

"Which room is Pooder in?"

"Number four, next to mine."

Kelly went to the next room and pounded on the door. When he got no answer, it was clear the boy had slipped out or had been taken.

"He sure was unsettled when we came in. He may have gone downstairs," Molly said.

Kelly nodded as the two of them started down the stairs. They stopped in the lobby, looked around, and, seeing nothing of Pooder, Molly became antsy.

"He ain't down here. I told him to sit tight, but he either didn't do what I said or he's been grabbed," Molly said, wringing her hands.

As they hurried outside, Kelly asked Molly if she'd had any dealings with a man named Alex Bond. Her face reddened.

"I, uh, well, to tell the truth, Abner was dealin' with a man of that name. He was supposed to invest in the mine for fifty thousand dollars, and I was to make him a partner."

"So, you never actually saw this man?"

"No. I trusted Abner to put the deal together. Then he goes and gets himself shot, and the boys lost the partnership letter I sent to Mr. Bond."

"So, as far as you know, this Bond never got the letter of agreement?"

"No, sir. And that means we're never goin' to see the money, neither, more's the pity." She hung her head and groaned. "I don't think we can save the mine without that money."

"What would you say if I told you we can save the mine, providing we find that gent who took Pooder?"

"I'd say you're a miracle worker. Do you really think there's a chance?"

"More than a chance, Molly, more than a chance. I need you to tell me everything you can about the deal Abner put together."

"All right. Well, this Bond was to send fifty thousand dollars to our bank to cover our debts just as soon as he received the letter agreeing to make him a partner in the mine. I sent it as he requested to Tucson, but it got lost, and now there won't be a deal, and the money won't be comin'. We'll lose the mine to our creditors. This was our last hope."

"How did you find out the mine was losing money?"

"Abner told me. He was our bookkeeper, and a fine one at that."

"I'm sorry to tell you this, Molly, but Abner wasn't the man you thought he was."

"What do you mean?"

"Abner Dillard and Alex Bond were working a scam. Abner was embezzling money from the mine over a period of time. When he had accrued enough, he contacted his partner, Bond, and then he told you about Bond's offer to save you. What he failed to tell you was that he intended to pull it off using your own money. As soon as he had part of the mine, you would have been let go, and he could reap the rewards of ownership without it costing him a plugged nickel."

"But the fifty thousand was to be used to pay off our debts," she said with dismay, nearly in tears.

"Abner had you worried about debts so you'd be an easy mark. There were no debts. The mine was doing fine in spite of his embezzlement. It was a scheme they'd played over and over with many different companies. Dillard would take money out of a company for a while, until he ran it into the ground by taking every penny he could, and then Bond would buy it up. He'd sometimes sell it off later and walk away a far richer man."

"I'm so stupid. How could I miss something so

obvious?" She shook her head as tears flowed down her red cheeks.

"You put your trust in Abner Dillard, a man who looked and acted honest. You're not stupid. You are a trusting soul, and that's nothing to be ashamed of."

"What will I do now?"

"First, I'm going to try to get your money back."

"What can I do to help?"

"Just stay here where you're safe, and I'll worry about the boys. Where would Pooder have gone, assuming he has yet to be found out?"

"I suppose he might have gone down to the livery to meet Blue."

Kelly and the Apache took off at a dead run.

Molly sat on an overstuffed leather couch in the lobby, put her head in her hands, and stared at the door, completely dejected. She was inwardly kicking herself for not knowing enough about the bookkeeping end of the business. That's why she'd hired Abner in the first place. He had presented himself as having left a large firm in St. Louis, moving to the southwest for his health. She'd bought his story, hook, line, and sinker. Now she was wondering what else she might have overlooked in her operation of the mine.

Halfway to the livery, Kelly and the Indian saw the boys racing toward them, hell-bent for leather.

Pooder hollered at the marshal as soon as he saw him. "He's right behind us, Marshal, and he intends to do us in!"

"I'll take care of him, boys. You go on down to the hotel and join Miss Molly. And whatever you do, stay put."

"We will, sir, guaranteed," Pooder whined. Blue was nodding his head in agreement.

When they got to the livery, the stranger was nowhere to be seen. Kelly was mulling over likely places for the man to go, when the Indian spoke up.

"New tracks on top of boys' go there." He pointed to the alleyway.

Kelly nodded as the Indian began tracking the fresh footprints all the way to the rear door of the Shot-to-Hell Saloon.

"I'll go around to the front. You come in from the back. You may have to cover me. No tellin' what this rattler might do when he sees a lawman."

Kelly turned and sprinted off for the saloon's front door.

As he nervously shuffled the deck of cards in front of him, the man stopped, instantly aware of the sound of footsteps behind him. Sensing danger, he spun out of his chair, almost getting his Remington clear of leather when he came face-to-face with the business end of Kelly's

Winchester. Almost, but not quite. The man eased his gun back into its holster and set the chair back on its legs after knocking it over in his haste to confront whoever had slipped up behind him. He sat back down.

"It ain't smart to sneak up behind a man. Who are you, and what do you want?" the man asked angrily. He picked up the deck of cards and began cutting it, turning over the bottom card, then replacing it. Kelly pulled his vest open to reveal his badge.

"I reckon I'm lookin' at the notorious Snake Torres, bounty hunter and murderer," the marshal said.

The man's eyes narrowed as his face contorted with inner rage at Kelly's accusation.

"How do you know me, and what right do you have callin' me a killer? I ain't done nothin' that could concern you."

"You and your partners attacked a ranch over near Cochise and killed the owner. His name was Alex Bond. I'd call *that* murder."

"I'd call it self-defense. He fired first. He shot my two friends after we rode out there to find out if he was really Alex Bowdre, a man wanted in New Mexico. Instead of talkin', he started throwin' lead at us. He shot both of them. I was lucky his rifle jammed as he was about to draw a bead on my head. I got him first."

"I figure it went a little further than that. First

off, you had no proof Bond was actually this Bowdre. Second, instead of getting out of there at the first shots and reporting the incident to the sheriff in Cochise, whose jurisdiction you were in, you took off with the bodies."

"Yeah, well, I didn't figure to get a warm reception from that old sheriff, anyway. Didn't think for one minute he'd believe me. It was my word against a dead man's, and I figured I'd hang for it. So I lit out."

"And that's all there was to it?"

"That's all."

"Not by a long shot, Snake. You found some information among Bond's papers that you figured to cash in on. So you decided to *become* Bond. You even stole some of his clothes and a pair of his boots, leaving your old ones behind."

"I don't know what you're talkin' about."

"Of course you do. And it might have worked, but you still had one more killin' in mind."

Once again, Snake's hand moved ever so slowly toward his revolver. If this conversation stayed on the track it seemed to be taking, Kelly knew that Torres likely wasn't going to be content to sit idly listening to a condemnation of his character—especially if it might lead to a rope-necktie party. Kelly wasn't oblivious to Snake's subtle attempt to draw his gun, but he didn't let on that he was on to the outlaw's intentions.

"What killin' would that be, Marshal?"

"The bookkeeper from the Gilded Lily Mine, Abner Dillard."

"Why would I want to kill this Dillard?"

"Because he could identify you as an imposter. He worked for Bond."

"You can't prove I killed anyone."

"I think I can. What say we walk over to your room at the hotel and look around? If, as I suspect, you have the money Dillard brought to town with him, that will be all the proof I need to put you away in Yuma Prison for a long time."

The moment of reckoning was upon him. Snake had to make a decision to either surrender peaceably or try shooting it out. The latter didn't seem smart, since the marshal was already pointing a rifle at him, but then, spending even a short time in Yuma held no appeal, either.

"I know what you're thinkin', Snake, but you don't have a chance. If I don't get you, my deputy will. He's right behind you with a rifle aimed at your gizzard. It's time to either make your play or drop your gun belt. What's it goin' to be?" Kelly thumbed back the Winchester's hammer for effect.

Snake Torres turned slightly in his chair. He could see that the marshal hadn't lied. The sight of an Apache sighting down a Spencer rifle sent a chill up his back. His time was running out. It was either die from a Winchester, accept a future locked away for the rest of his life in Yuma

Prison, or get hanged for shooting Abner Dillard.

Snake Torres had shot many a man, mostly in the back or under circumstances that could only be termed as squarely in his favor. He wasn't very brave, but he saw the reality of his present position clearly. Three choices, none anything to look forward to. He squirmed for a moment before making that fateful decision.

Sheriff Hawk Burns burst through the swinging doors before the smoke had cleared. He was met with the sight of yet another corpse for him to contend with. He shook his head and mumbled something about wishing the marshal would take his Indian friend and light a shuck out of Desert Belle, and the sooner the better.

Piedmont Kelly and Spotted Dog eased out of the saloon without a word and headed for the hotel to get Molly McQueen's money back for her. And, in the process, maybe have a talk with a couple of young men about responsibility and what to do with it when it's bestowed on you.

Chapter Thirty

Things hadn't gone exactly as the marshal would have preferred, all things considered, but he could sleep at night. Molly's self-recrimination at being duped so completely by Abner Dillard was going to be hard to put behind her. Even the president of the Desert Belle Bank and Trust had reassured her there was little she could have done differently. "After all," he said, "not everybody is good with ciphering. Why, I was fooled by that scrawny bookkeeper, myself."

The whole affair wasn't over for Piedmont Kelly, however. In Bond's papers he'd found a number of other businesses that had been swindled out of their bank accounts by the clever pair. He felt a need to try to set things right, or as much as he could. And he would get started on that formidable task as soon as he got back to Cochise. He would also be seeking elucidation to the one unanswered question that had nagged him almost from the start.

Even Spotted Dog could tell that the marshal was still unsettled by the events of the past few days. As far as he knew, however, there was nothing more to puzzle over except his own immediate future. Did the marshal no longer need his help?

Kelly noticed the Apache's uneasiness. He figured it must be unsettling to him to know he had to go back to San Carlos. But Kelly also knew it was best that Spotted Dog be back with his own people. The Indian had saved his life twice in almost as many days, and that would be hard to repay, if not impossible. Halfway between Desert Belle and Cochise, Kelly reined in. He reached into his saddlebags and pulled out a small leather bag of silver dollars.

"This is where we split up, old friend. I'll miss havin' you around to watch my back. But I can assure you, it won't be the last time I call on you for help. But here's something to help make things a little easier at San Carlos." He tossed the bag to the Apache.

"I help friend whenever he need."

"Thank you, Spotted Dog."

The Indian started to unpin the badge Kelly had given him.

Kelly held up a hand. "You keep it. You'll need it again sometime, I'm sure. It would be a good idea to put it away where no one else knows you have it, though."

Spotted Dog grunted and held up his Spencer in salute, then rode off toward the reservation with a whoop. Kelly sat for several minutes watching the Indian disappear into the brush, quietly wishing that society was ready for alliances of this sort as a normal course of life. He had heard about Judge Isaac Parker up in Fort Smith hiring both blacks *and* Indians as deputy marshals to go into the Indian Territories to keep the peace. *If it works there, maybe it'll work here someday too.*

"Somethin' perplexin' you, Piedmont?" asked Sheriff John Henry Stevens. "You been fidgetin' in that chair for an hour."

"Yep. It's bothered me from the start, as soon as I heard about that letter Molly McQueen sent."

"What's the problem? It never got into the hands of those who could hold her to it, did it?"

"No, but why did Alex Bond want it sent to Tucson, when it would have been easier to pick it up here in Cochise?"

"Hmm. Good question. Sorry, son, but I got no answer for how the outlaw mind works. Far as I'm concerned, you put a stop to them owlhoots' scheme, and that's that. Let 'er go."

Kelly pushed out of his chair and sauntered to the door. "I'm goin' for a bite to eat. See you later." He headed straight for Nettie's.

"Why, you can't fool me. It ain't even time for dinner yet, and—" He found he was talking to the wind. He shook his head and went back to cleaning his Colt, pieces of which he had strewn

281

all over the top of his desk, along with some brushes and strips of cloth.

Nettie greeted Piedmont with an eager smile and motioned him to a table not far from the kitchen. "You'll be closer this way. I can keep an eye on you, so's you don't slip out before sayin' good-bye like you did the last time."

"I was kinda in a hurry then. Those papers of Bond's held the secret to his scheme to steal another business, which it appears he'd done several times before."

"Is it possible to get any of the money back for the people he scammed?"

"If we can get a judge to open Bond's bank account and declare it available for restitution. Depends on whether he's got family somewhere. It's a long shot, but I have to try."

"Then it's all over, and you can rest up here a while, or at least until some other sidewinder decides to test your mettle. Meanwhile, I'll make sure you're well fed." She gave him a coy wink.

"I *suppose* it's behind me," he said, without his usual confidence.

"What do you mean? Sounds like you think there's more to it."

"I keep struggling with why Bond wanted the deed sent to Tucson instead of here. That's all. It's probably nothing."

"Did Bond normally get mail here? Did he have a box? Doesn't make sense to go all the way to Tucson when he could ride into Cochise to complete his nefarious scheme. Probably did it many times, and we just weren't aware of his activities."

Kelly rubbed his chin. She could tell by his silent searching that he didn't know the answer. The expression on his face told her he thought he should have, though. Her suspicions were confirmed when he suddenly jumped up and rushed out the door with only a "That's it!"

He hurried down the street toward the post office. She watched from her front window as he entered the tiny clapboard building, then, a minute later, exited. But he didn't come straight back as she figured he would. *Where's he off to now?* She sighed and went back to the kitchen to clean up from the lunch customers. *That man's like a dust devil—never know when he's going to blow in or when he's goin' to just disappear into thin air.*

It was almost an hour later when Kelly wandered back to Nettie's with a grin on his face. She wasn't entirely sure she wanted to quiz him about where he'd been, since the last time she'd asked him a question, he took off like he'd been snake-bit. She decided it might be better to let him come clean of his own accord. But could she curtail her own natural curiosity?

When he came in, he strode boldly into the kitchen, took her by the shoulders, and kissed her hard. It took her a second to get her breath and twice as long to wipe the surprised smile off her face. He turned and went casually back out to the dining room and took a seat near the window, almost as if he'd never left.

Wiping her soapy hands on a towel, she came over to his table and sat down across from him, clearly puzzled. "Dare I ask what *that* was all about?"

"That was a down payment for your help in solving the Alex Bond situation. You have a mighty good head on your shoulders, Nettie, and a pretty one too."

Nettie blushed. "Thank you. But what does that have to do with this fella, Bond?"

"You were right. Bond *did* have a post office box right here in Cochise, and he regularly received mail from many different places. So I went to the telegraph office and sent a wire to the postmaster in Tucson. And, just as I thought, he'd never heard of an Alex Bond."

"You act as if that's good news." She leaned her elbows on the table and put her chin in her hands. Her questioning frown made him snicker.

"It *is* good news. The whole thing makes sense now."

"What makes sense? C'mon, out with it. Uh,

wait a minute. If Bond didn't have a box in Tucson, then why send that letter there, right?"

"That's right. There *was,* however, a box held in the name of Abner Dillard. It was the same number that Molly addressed the letter to."

"So, the mine's bookkeeper sent it to himself?"

"Uh-huh. Only he didn't want the mine. He already had what he wanted: the fifty thousand dollars he'd embezzled. That and he didn't want Bond to find out that he'd pulled a fast one on him. Dillard was probably tired of doing the work, taking all the risk, and getting a pittance for his efforts. By cutting Bond out of the picture, he figured to just disappear. No one would know why he'd left, and he'd doctored the books so well, it would be a long time before anyone was able to figure it out. He was free and clear. He was waiting in Desert Belle, not for Bond to arrive to make the switch, but for the next stage out of town."

"But that Snake fella got to him first and killed him?"

"Yep."

"Do you suppose Dillard ever knew that Bond was dead all along?"

"I don't see how he could have. I didn't even know for sure, although I had my suspicions when I noticed a pair of badly scuffed boots and a pair of dirty jeans and shirt tossed in the corner of an otherwise neat and orderly bedroom at Bond's place. They didn't fit."

"Snake must have caught on to Bond's scheme."

"I figure he rifled the man's office before taking off. He probably put it all together and decided to get rid of his two dead partners as well as Bond in such a way that no one would know what had happened at the ranch. It was easy to adopt Bond's identity, at least for a while."

"Pretty clever."

"Would have been if Snake Torres had thought about it a little longer. If he had, he'd have known that at some point he'd have to prove he had at least a little business savvy. He would have been found out sooner or later. I figure it must have been pride or something like it that told him he could line his pockets with even more of the Gilded Lily's money. Greed can be a powerful quick trip to hell. He should have taken the fifty thousand and skipped out immediately."

Nettie sat back, bewildered by how convoluted the whole thing sounded. And how many evil people seemed to inhabit the frontier. After her close call at the hands of Sheriff Drago and his scoundrel deputy, Cloyd, she'd hoped never to see or hear of such miscreants again.

"Coffee?" Nettie asked.

"I've got a better idea. How about you close up

early and I take you to the hotel dining room? You could use a night off."

Her eyes lit up at the prospect of being out with Piedmont Kelly somewhere other than in her own restaurant.

"I can be ready in ten minutes," she said as she disappeared into the back room. She reappeared without her apron. She'd put a couple of new combs into her hair and draped a frilly pink shawl around her shoulders.

The smile on Kelly's face said he approved.

Center Point Large Print
600 Brooks Road / PO Box 1
Thorndike ME 04986-0001 USA

(207) 568-3717

US & Canada:
1 800 929-9108
www.centerpointlargeprint.com